M000043479

JEROBOAM DERANGEMENT SYNDROME

A HEBREW SCHOLAR'S DREAM OF FOX NEWS HOSTING ISRAEL'S MOST MALIGNED KING, TRUMP TWIN, JEROBOAM BEN NEBAT

SIEGFRIED JOHNSON

©2019 Siegfried Johnson. All rights reserved. No part of this publication may be reproduced, distributed, or transmitted in any form or by any means, including photocopying, recording, or other electronic or mechanical methods, without the prior written permission of the author, except in the case of brief quotations embodied in critical reviews and certain other noncommercial uses permitted by copyright law.

ISBN: 978-1-54397-489-8 (print)
ISBN: 978-1-54397-490-4 (ebook)

INTRODUCTION

———

Nearly three thousand years ago, in 930 B. C., a successful business leader of real estate projects in Jerusalem rode a populist wave to the summit of political power in Israel. As Solomon's globalist-oriented reign neared its end, conflicting tribal concerns at home were increasingly polarizing the country, ripening conditions for a political leader to emerge from outside the nation's established royalty.

After a stunning ascension to the throne, aided by the interference of a powerful leader of a foreign government, Pharaoh Shishak of Egypt, this new king moved into his palace with his beautiful, foreign-born, multi-lingual wife. Moving quickly to enact commonsense policies gleaned from his experiences in the non-political world, he set out to fulfill his Israel-first promises by lifting the burden placed on the people by his predecessor's regime.

Of supreme importance to this king was the building of his "Wall." In an act of national protectionism, he built virtual walls on his northern and southern borders by erecting pilgrimage shrines in Dan and Bethel. Aimed at slowing the flow of pilgrims across the border to Solomon's temple, this new king's "Wall" forever earned the scorn of the Jerusalem-based Establishment known as the House of David.

Though successful in bettering his people's lives, ruling for twenty-two years and setting Israel on a course which would endure for over two centuries, this "Father" of a nation was unrelentingly maligned by the Establishment's prophets and scribes, seeing in this king a core corruption overshadowing the significant accomplishments of his administration.

This king's name was Jeroboam ben Nebat. The following eight passages from 1 and 2 Kings, a running commentary on the reigns of Israel's kings spanning two centuries, each condemn subsequent kings of Israel for refusing to reverse Jeroboam's "Wall" policy, a clear indication of how deeply Judah's historians were inflicted with *Jeroboam Derangement Syndrome.*

Israel's 6th King: Omri

Omri did evil in the sight of the LORD . . .

For he walked in all the ways of Jeroboam ben Nebat and in his sins which he made Israel sin,

provoking the LORD God of Israel with their idols.

(1 Kings 16:25-26)

Israel's 8th King: Ahaziah

Ahaziah . . . did evil in the sight of the LORD and walked in the way of his father and in the way of his mother and in the way of Jeroboam ben Nebat who caused Israel to sin.

(1 Kings 22:51-52)

Israel's 10th King: Jehu

So Jehu destroyed Baal worship in Israel. However, he did not turn away from the sins of Jeroboam ben Nebat, which he had caused Israel to commit—the worship of the golden calves at Bethel and Dan . . . He did not turn away from the sins of Jeroboam . . .

(2 Kings 10:28-31)

Israel's 11th King: Jehoahaz

Jehoahaz, son of Jehu . . . did evil in the eyes of the LORD by following the sins of Jeroboam ben Nebat, which he had caused Israel to commit, and he did not turn away from them.

So the LORD's anger burned against Israel.

(2 Kings 13:1-3)

Israel's 12th King: Jehoash

Jehoash son of Jehoahaz . . . did evil in the eyes of the LORD and did not turn away from any of the sins of Jeroboam ben Nebat, which he had caused Israel to commit; he continued in them.

(2 Kings 13:10-11)

Israel's 13th King: Zechariah

Zechariah . . . did evil in the eyes of the LORD, *as his predecessors had done. He did not turn away from the sins of Jeroboam ben Nebat, which he had caused Israel to commit.*

(2 Kings 15:8-9)

Israel's 15th King: Menahem

Menahem . . . did evil in the eyes of the LORD. *During his entire reign he did not turn away from the sins of Jeroboam ben Nebat, which he had caused Israel to commit.*

(2 Kings 15:17-18)

Israel's 16th King: Pekahiah

Pekahiah did evil in the eyes of the LORD. *He did not turn away from the sins of Jeroboam ben Nebat, which he had caused Israel to commit.*

(2 Kings 15:23-24)

Israel's final fall is blamed on its first king, Jeroboam ben Nebat

When he had torn Israel from the house of David, they made Jeroboam ben Nebat king. Jeroboam drove Israel from following the LORD and made them commit great sin.

The people of Israel continued in all the sins that Jeroboam committed: they did not depart from them until the LORD removed Israel out of his sight, as he had foretold through all his servants the prophets. So Israel was exiled from their own land to Assyria until this day.

(2 Kings 17:21-23)

A WORD FROM THE AUTHOR

———

One of my most anticipated afternoon pleasures in these never dull days of the Trump presidency is to arrive home in time to pour a glass of red and watch *The Five*, especially enjoying the spotlight shone on the day's latest instances of *Trump Derangement Syndrome*.

As a student of Hebrew language and literature with post-graduate degrees from Mid-America Baptist Theological Seminary (Memphis, 1984) and the University of Michigan's Department of Near Eastern Studies (Ann Arbor, 1989), I've long been fascinated by a similar phenomenon in the time of Jeroboam ben Nebat, the first king of the ten tribes breaking away from Jerusalem's House of David.

Despite founding a nation which endured for two centuries, this king from outside the royal Establishment was viciously treated by the prophets and scribes who, as the ancient world's primary brokers of influence, functioned as the equivalent of today's media, they the lens through which the people learned of government, religious, and cultural life. I suggest that what this media class offered their listeners may be read as *Jeroboam Derangement Syndrome*, incredibly parallel to the *Trump Derangement Syndrome* infecting today's mainstream media.

Bible readers are introduced to Jeroboam in 1 Kings 11:26, a genealogical note to which is added a brief statement of his sedition: "*Jeroboam ben Nebat, an Ephraimite of Zeredah, a servant of Solomon, whose mother's name was Zeruah, a widow, rebelled against the king.*"

Learning of Jeroboam's political ambitions, Solomon unsuccessfully sought to have him assassinated, resulting in his flight to Egypt. Once there, he was embraced by Pharaoh Shishak and made a royal by marrying his daughter, Princess Ano, a relationship which would prove fruitful for both the pharaoh and for Israel's future king.

After Solomon's death, Jeroboam returned from exile to lead a delegation from the ten tribes to Shechem, where he presented a list of grievances to Solomon's son and anointed successor, Rehoboam. When the new king refused to address their complaints, instead promising more of the same Solomonic policies of inequitable taxation and conscripted labor that had buried Israel's tribes under a heavy economic burden, Jeroboam led ten tribes to separate from the House of David. Violence erupted with the assassination of a representative of Rehoboam's Labor Department, Adoram, sent to quell the unrest. Rehoboam's reaction was to choose flight over fight. As he rushed back to safety within Jerusalem's walls, walls partially built by Jeroboam himself, a hastily called assembly of the ten tribes proclaimed Jeroboam ben Nebat as their new king.

Like Donald Trump, Jeroboam was a charismatic figure whose pre-political life was that a skilled builder and real estate developer. Identified by Solomon as a leader with extraordinary promise, he was invited into Solomon's administration as a director of the labor forces conscripted from the northern tribes. One of Jeroboam's most heralded projects, mentioned in the 1 Kings narrative, was called the Millo, a wall which has been unearthed and identified so that it is viewed today by tourists in Jerusalem's *'ir David*, the City of David.

It's no wonder that Flavius Josephus, the 1st century Jewish-Roman historian, described Jeroboam's work in Solomon's administration as *"curator of the walls"* of Jerusalem. Nor is it any wonder that, once declared king, Jeroboam did what he knew best. He built walls. His highest priority was to build what may be regarded as Jeroboam's "Wall" by erecting cultic shrines in Dan and Bethel (near his northern and southern borders), a protectionist move to eliminate the need for pilgrimages to Jerusalem, thereby lessening the threat of a reversal of tribal allegiances to King Rehoboam and the House of David. Seen as rivals to Solomon's temple, these shrines moved to fury Jerusalem's "Deep State" Establishment, Judah's historians coming unhinged with Jeroboam-hatred as they describe king after king after doomed king through Israel's 200 years as *"doing evil in the eyes of the LORD, not turning from the sins of Jeroboam ben Nebat which he caused Israel to sin."*

Thirty years ago I wrote a thesis in Ann Arbor on the Jeroboam narrative titled *"Doomed from the Start,"* pointing out how the Bible's historians, while reluctantly accepting the legitimacy of Jeroboam's reign as a turning of divine providence, yet regarded the north's demise

200 years later as the inevitable outcome of a nation doomed from the start by the unconscionable acts of its corrupt first leader.

Not only had Jeroboam built his "Wall," he sought also to "Drain the Swamp," appointing priests from outside the accepted pool of Levites. This further infuriated the Establishment scribes who, conflating the nation's end with its beginning, its *Dusk* with its *Dawn*, blamed Israel's final fall on Jeroboam ben Nebat, the nation's Father who had lived fully two centuries earlier.

In the media's treatment of President Trump, whose campaign motto ("*Make America Great Again!*") echoes the Hebrew meaning of Jeroboam's name ("*May the people be great!*"), I've observed parallels which will be highlighted in these pages. Mainstream media narratives often come unhinged with Trump-hatred, describing his presidency, no matter the solid list of policy achievements domestic and foreign, as *Doomed from the Start.*

In their rise to power both Jeroboam ben Nebat and Donald J. Trump triggered shocking moments in their nation's history. Jeroboam's ascension was a populist reaction of the ten tribes to the prospect of Solomon's son, Rehoboam, continuing his father's policies. Trump's astounding White House win was likewise a populist reaction to the prospect of Hillary Clinton's continuation of the policies of Barack Obama, voters in effect denying Obama a third term.

Just as the weaker Rehoboam following Solomon opened the door to an unexpected leader from outside the Establishment, so the weaker candidate anointed to follow Obama swung open the door for a non-Establishment candidate from outside the club of Republican insiders vying for the nomination. Few dreamed Trump could win that nomination, much less the White House. The thought of such a prospect was at first was a joke welcomed with gusto by media and political personalities, not perceiving how very weak and unlikeable Obama's successor candidate was, nor how frustrated the people had become with his administration's policies.

What I offer here, at the intersection of a political conservative with a scholar of Hebrew language and history, is my imagining of a dream in which Jeroboam ben Nebat and his family appear as special guests on Fox News' hit late afternoon show, *The Five*. In my dream, King Jeroboam is joined by Nebat (his father), Zeruah (his mother), and Ano (his wife). In the fifth spot I've placed an outlier to offer a contrary view, the prophet from Shiloh who aided Jeroboam in his rise to power, only to flip by predicting and endorsing his downfall.

I hope readers will find my dream, based on the biblical story of one of the most disruptive and pivotal figures in Israel's history, to be informative, insightful, and entertaining as comparisons are drawn between King Jeroboam and President Trump, Queen Ano and First Lady Melania Trump, King Solomon and President Obama, Rehoboam and Hillary, and more.

For those who enjoy the stories of the Bible, perhaps my telling of the Jeroboam narrative in Midrashic fashion, imaginatively treating the text as the beginning rather than the end of the story by inviting the characters to come alive and speak in first person, will lead to a closer reading of the Bible's narrative of this unexpected and much-loathed king.

Jeroboam's story is not nearly as widely known as such luminaries of Hebrew history as Abraham, Moses, David, or Solomon. Yet, while one searches in vain for books or films given to Jeroboam's life, his is a sensational story worth telling, especially in these unprecedented days of the Trump presidency. My dream, offering Jeroboam ben Nebat as a doppelganger of President Donald J. Trump, draws intriguing parallels between today's political climate and a time 3,000 years ago when another successful builder unexpectedly grabbed the reins of government, his unconventional actions creating a certain *Jeroboam Anxiety Disorder* throughout the mainstream, a disorder of disdain easily discernible in the biblical narrative.

For political conservatives who, like me, are daily amused at the seemingly ceaseless stream of commentary from the Left identified as *Trump Derangement Syndrome*, I hope my dream will speak to today's political climate as much as it does to that time when the once United Kingdoms of David and Solomon split into the two nations of Judah and Israel.

As a student of Hebrew and a long-time pastor, I am a biblical scholar claiming no expertise as a political commentator. Yet, who could help in today's political climate but wonder if a deeply divided America is following a similar tribal path down a dark road toward division? To this end, I mean for the image of *Dawn* and *Dusk,* a recurring theme in my dream, to be a vessel in which to offer political commentary, addressing the question of whether these United States can be far from a *Dusk* that will close the bright day of the American experiment whose *Dawn* was over twenty-four decades ago.

Might the Leftist, progressive areas of our country along its coastal corridors and populated urban areas be the new Judah, backed whole-heartedly by the Establishment's media? Conversely, might the flyover states of middle America be akin to Israel's ten breakaway tribes, a group surprisingly maintaining political clout even while losing the popular vote by ever wider margins, thanks to the wisdom of the Founders in establishing the Electoral College? Perhaps Jeroboam and his family, with the help of *The Five's* hosts, can help us grapple with those and more questions.

John Bunyan's literary masterpiece, *The Pilgrim's Progress*, opens: "*As I walked through the wilderness of this world, I lighted on a certain place where was a Den, and I laid me down in that place to sleep: and, as I slept, I dreamed a dream. I dreamed, and behold, I saw . . .*"

With apologies to Bunyan, I begin: "*As I walked through the wilderness of the Trump presidency, I lighted on a certain recliner in my den with a glass of red and, as I watched The Five and became Cabernet drowsy, I dreamed a dream. I dreamed, and behold, I saw . . .*"

I invite you to settle back, pour a glass of your favorite beverage, and join me for *The Five*, coming on just now with Greg Gutfeld's opening monologue:

CHAPTER ONE

"Doomed from the Start"
(A Gutfeld monologue)

————

Good afternoon, America, I'm Greg Gutfeld with Dana Perino, Jesse Watters, Juan Williams, and Jedediah Bila. It's five o'clock in New York and this is a special edition of *The Five.*

Let's recap. A wildly successful leader in real estate development, his center of business in his country's largest metropolitan area, emerges on the political scene from out of nowhere, as if a gift from heaven descending a golden escalator. This star from a constellation far outside the usual cast of political luminaries is at first regarded as a joke. He's hilarious! Well, hilarious until his movement began to gather momentum, filling rallies with excited supporters drawn to his promises to build a wall and to drain the swamp.

After this celebrity stuns the world with victory, he moves into his capital city with his foreign-born, multi-lingual wife, a woman intelligent, beautiful, and so shy as to barely speak a word. Entirely lacking in presidential demeanor and utterly devoid of politically correct speech he may be, but the lack of those things contributes to his image as a fighter, a quality as adored by his supporters as it is abhorred by the political Establishment and mainstream media.

Once in office he systematically begins to unravel the economic burden placed on the people by the previous administration. He moves immediately to keep his promises, raising workers' hopes by lowering taxes and rolling back the economy-dampening policies of his predecessor. With a businessman-turned-politician at the helm, the economy begins to hum.

A self-described nationalist determined to put his country first in all things, one of his greatest passions is to build a wall on his border, an anti-globalist idea further infuriating his enemies in the Deep State. Wasting no time, he begins to drain the swamp by removing Establishment figures from important posts and placing political outsiders in power. As the Establishment and mainstream media sense that they are losing their grip on power, they spew vitriol in a torrent of Fake News aimed at bringing down their newly elected head of state. Stunned by the loss of their anointed candidate, they propose that such a shocking defeat could only have happened with the meddling of a powerful leader from a foreign government, seeking further to de-legitimize their new head of state.

Now, I ask *The Five's* viewers, have I just described President Donald J. Trump? If you wish, but actually what I've described is the political situation of 3,000 years ago as told in the Hebrew Bible, a.k.a. the Old Testament. This king's name, whose rise to political stardom is eerily reminiscent of Donald J. Trump, is Jeroboam ben Nebat.

Welcome to a special two-hour episode in which we've not only doubled our time, but for the first time ever we've doubled our number. Today we are not *The Five* but *The Ten*. Seated by each of us today through the magic of television is a figure from the Hebrew Bible's story of Jeroboam ben Nebat, who three millennia ago led "*The Ten*" tribes to split off from Jerusalem's political Establishment, known as the House of David.

"*Jeroboam who?*" you ask. Jeroboam the son of Nebat, that's who. You may not know his story as well as other biblical figures such as Abraham and Isaac, Moses and Joshua, David and Solomon, but Jeroboam ben Nebat was the father of a new nation, the northern ten tribes of Israel. Why would such an important biblical figure be less known than the aforementioned biblical luminaries? Maybe because like our own president, Donald J. Trump, he was passionately despised by a Deep State Establishment going to extremes to malign his name.

While the parallels between Jeroboam and Trump are uncanny, I have it on good authority that Trump's middle initial, J, does NOT stand for Jeroboam. Still, the similarities you will hear tonight are astounding. Both were successful businessmen heading massive real estate projects. Both came from out of nowhere to reach the pinnacle of political power. Both moved into their capitals with foreign, multi-lingual wives.

Both rolled back the policies of their predecessor, stoking immediate economic revival. Both promised to build a wall, and Jeroboam did just that, a virtual wall, anyway. The shrines which Jeroboam built in the north and the south functioned as walls aimed at putting the brakes on the flow of pilgrims crossing the border. Jeroboam's "Wall" functioned successfully, as planned, but at the same time released streams of rage from the mouths and pens of the Establishment's prophets and scribes.

Nor is that all. Both were accused of profiting from foreign entanglements. Jeroboam's rise to power was, in fact, assisted by the major power to the south, Pharaoh Shishak of Egypt, who made him a royal by arranging for his daughter to become Mrs. Jeroboam. Her name is Ano, Queen Ano, and you will have the opportunity to meet her this evening.

Finally, both were immediately resisted and thoroughly rejected by the Deep State, which considered their administrations *Doomed from the Start.* You ask how could we possibly know all of this about a king from 3,000 years ago? True, we don't have access to ancient archives of *The Jerusalem Times*, but we do know who the influence peddlers of that day were and what they wrote about Jeroboam, screaming hysterically about his dual sins of building a wall and draining the swamp. Prophets and scribes they were called, their words fashioning the story that biblical history has told of Jeroboam and his family.

But today – talk about a world exclusive! – you'll hear their story from their own mouths, a story that, for the first time offered to any audience, will fill in the lacunae, those massive gaps between the verses of the biblical text and their actual experiences told in their own words.

You'll hear tonight how as a young man Jeroboam's potential was noticed by none other than King Solomon who, seeing in Jeroboam a man of means and extremely capable, enlisted this rising star by appointing him to what we might today call an Under-Secretary in Solomon's Department of Labor.

Another had taken notice of the young man, and he is with us tonight to tell his story. Ahijah the prophet of Shiloh encountered the young builder near Jerusalem and whispered that God had rejected Solomon and had chosen him instead to be king over the northern ten tribes. Solomon, through his spies, heard those whispers and tried to have Jeroboam assassinated. The attempt was unsuccessful, but a close enough shave to send Jeroboam running to Egypt.

That's where foreign collusion enters the story. Jeroboam had not escaped Pharaoh's notice, either. Egypt was interested, then as now, in the politics of their neighbor to the north. Pharaoh saw in Jeroboam a potential friend of tremendous future worth and became instrumental in raising his status, validating his royal credentials by giving him his own daughter, Ano, in marriage, their romance adding a real-life element to the story which the Bible neglects to report. The princess married a commoner in no way common, better positioning him for his future challenge to the throne.

When Solomon died a few years later his son, Rehoboam, couldn't muster the political clout to hold the nation together. The ten tribes made Jeroboam king, and he proceeded immediately to build his wall, something the seething scribes of the swamp saw as an unforgiveable scandal. The outrage intensified when Jeroboam overlooked the

Establishment priests of the Levites, appointing outsiders to the power-ful priestly positions having oversight of his wall.

No wonder the verdict pronounced over and over by the Deep State is a delirious case of *Jeroboam Derangement Syndrome*, his name surfacing throughout Israel's 200+ year history as the casus belli of divine displeasure, king after king described as *"doing evil in the sight of the Lord, not turning from the sins of Jeroboam ben Nebat, which he caused Israel to sin."*

So let's get to it! With us today on *The Five* is King Jeroboam himself, who will make the case that he was unfairly treated by the Establishment media, his accomplishments ignored and his name unfairly dragged as a carcass through Hebrew history.

Wasn't it his predecessor Solomon who asked, *"Is anything new under the sun?"* Like Trump, Jeroboam entered the political fray by presenting himself as the one who could and would address the griev-ances of those forgotten by an entrenched royalty which had lost touch with the real-life struggles of the people. These forgotten, who had shouldered the burden of Solomon's economic policies based on his globalist ambitions, were promised only more of the same by his son Rehoboam, setting the stage for the rise of a nationalist outsider who was a no-nonsense, don't-give-a-damn-about-political-correctness businessman. Sound familiar?

It's not just Donald Trump's presidency that liberals now deem *Doomed from the Start*. The radical Left has been emboldened to become more honest about who they've always been, dropping the façade of being moderates and much more openly embracing socialism.

"Trump? Yes, a scoundrel, but he's merely a symptom of, not the cause of, our disease. The Donald is but the latest manifestation of a problem that began with The George! It's the Father our country who set in motion the ills we see today, despite our nation's 243 year history."

For the radical Left, the entire American experiment was *Doomed from the Start*, the seeds of doom planted from the beginning in a Constitution written by slave owners, in the evils of free market capitalism, in the right to bear arms, in the arrogant idea of American exceptionalism and, of course, by daring to enforce its borders. All these odious things long preceded Donald J. Trump. The country was hopelessly flawed from the get-go and must pay for its original sins.

Doomed from the Start! Am I talking about Israel ten centuries before Christ, or America twenty centuries after Christ? I can't tell! As Governor Cuomo said, *"He's not going to Make America Great Again. It was never that great."* He may as well have said, *"Let's put the blame where it really belongs. Not on The Donald, as despicable as he is, but on The George!"*

Ludicrous? Precisely that, my friends, is what happened to our special guest. Jeroboam ben Nebat was the father of the ten tribes of Israel, yet on him was laid the fault for his country's demise 200 years later! Hebrew historians couldn't let go of what they saw as something rotten at the core of the Jeroboam administration, despite the fact that his "Wall" policy was so successful that no king, not one king in the nation's two century and twenty-two king history, ever reversed it.

This evening we'll hear that story from Jeroboam and his family. In the first hour your hosts will fade into the background so that we can all become familiar with this ancient story through their own words, words that will take us between and beyond the verses of the Bible.

In the second hour, Dana, Jesse, Juan, Jedediah, and I will probe their perspective on our own president, talk about President Trump's utter rejection by the Establishment and mainstream media, and learn what they think about America's path into the future.

So with that, today we welcome to *"The Five"* five more. Tonight we are *"The Ten,"* an appropriate number, since we're talking about the ten tribes which crowned Jeroboam king.

Sitting by me is Nebat, Jeroboam's father. Dana's special guest is the mother of Jeroboam, Zeruah. At center stage, Jesse has the honor of hosting the king himself. Beside Juan is the one guest not of the royal family but key to his story, one who will no doubt bring a different perspective, just as Juan does daily on *The Five*. I'm talking about the prophet Ahijah of Shiloh, who first identified Jeroboam as the future king then withdrew his support, flipping to the other side. Finally, sitting by Jedediah is Jeroboam's Egyptian wife, Ano.

We begin with Nebat, the father of King Jeroboam. Welcome, sir, and thanks for being a part of what is today, *The Ten*.

CHAPTER TWO

Nebat, the father of Jeroboam

Shalom aleichem, Greg, and *shalom* to my American friends. It's an honor to visit with you today. You live in a most blessed country, a great country, I dare say, despite living in a time of such rancor. It was just so in my country during my short lifetime 3,000 years ago.

Ours was a blessed country too, great and proud. Our greatness, though, anchored as it was in our Hebrew culture, was fast fading under Solomon, despite what you may have read to the contrary in the Bible, which is, of course, the "mainstream" media narrative fashioning your understanding of the times in which I lived. Israel needed a new leader who, after Solomon, would "Make Israel Great Again."

Your viewers will surely not be shocked by my opinion that, in the same way, America's greatness was intentionally diminished by President Obama's determination to "fundamentally transform

America," mainstream media narratives notwithstanding. Just as after Solomon Israel needed a leader to "Make Israel Great Again," so the American people responded instinctively to the need, after Obama, to "Make America Great Again."

Solomon, you see, had chosen to open wide the borders, enthusiastically embracing other cultures and making accommodations for the practice of their faiths. Such diversity, which in your time is considered the peak of morality, was soundly condemned by our prophets. We were taught that opening the door to foreign cultures with their gods and goddesses was dangerous, an influence sure to erode our attachments to our God, he with the unspeakable Name of the tetragrammaton, Baruch ha-Shem (Blessed be the Name!).

Just as with Obama, King Solomon's actions, while popular on the global stage, wore away at our cultural integrity. The prophets condemned his building of *bamot*, meaning, "high places." These were cultic sites honoring the gods of the *goyim*, the gentiles. As a politician his real interest, of course, was not to honor their gods so much as to make friends of the followers of those gods. Making friends is what politicians do. What they must do, I suppose, build alliances. Solomon was expert in that field, accounting for his large harem of wives and concubines, each one evidence of his many political entanglements on the global stage.

You will hear the prophet tonight declare that Solomon's accommodation of other cultures was the reason for God's anger, the reason Yahweh split Solomon's kingdom and gave ten tribes to my son. So be it, but if Solomon's globalism was the cause of God's anger, you need to know that the anger of the people which brought my son to power was caused by something else entirely. Our concern wasn't at all religious, but rather intensely practical and economic. Solomon's globalist ambitions, while lifting his reputation on the world stage, was making our people losers at home, in the villages where they lived. We were hurting, and he didn't care. He, in fact, was the cause of our hurting, caring only for his own reputation in the community of nations surrounding Israel.

Like Obama, Solomon was a darling of a king on the global stage, amassing no shortage of accolades and even the swooning of foreign leaders, not to mention the press. The Queen of Sheba is the example you will surely know best, she left breathless at the sight of Solomon's glory, both his much-vaunted wisdom and his enormous wealth. This phenomenon I witnessed again with your media's sycophantic treatment of Obama, tingling sensations amid the glitter of the words spoken by fawning media personalities.

But, and again like Obama, in economic terms Solomon was much less successful. While in no way stagnant, neither was the economy booming or even nearly living up to its potential. To me the word "populist" to describe either my son's ascension to power or that of your current president, Mr. Trump, simply affirms that people were ready for a change, after both Solomon and Obama. As President Trump represents change in your day, it was my son, Jeroboam, who brought change to Israel after Solomon. So, thank-you, Greg, and thank-you to *The Five* for the opportunity to tell our side of the story, the first time it shall have been told in three millennia.

Forgive me, it seems I've already said much without formally introducing myself. My name is Nebat, the father of Israel's most famous posthumously born child, whom you know as Jeroboam ben Nebat. I love your word *posthumous*, a hybrid meaning "*coming after*" (posterus) the "*ground*" (humus). That's my son, the posthumously-born-one who came into the world only after his *abba*, his daddy, had been planted into the ground. Forgive my indelicacy, but at my son's birth my flesh was rapidly decomposing, four months dead.

Were it not for my son you would never have known my name, yet my name lives. My impact on history began only after I was gathered with my ancestors into *'eretz ha-kadosh*, the sacred earth, my broken skull bearing the mark of blunt force trauma to the head, the result of a blow from one of Solomon's soldiers.

My son, ben Nebat, would become the first king of the ten northern tribes known as Israel or, often, Ephraim. I prefer Ephraim. I can't take credit for much in my son's life, but at least I can take credit for his tribal heritage. That I gave him, and proudly. Jeroboam ben Nebat, the Ephraimite, the pride of our village, Zeredah.

How I wish I had known him, but I died just past midway through my wife's pregnancy. You know her as Zeruah, though I called her, simply, Zer. I smile at the mention of her name, itself quite the story, but it's her story, so I'll leave it to Zer to share it with you. I know she will.

I died a young man, 23 years old, killed by a soldier sent to our village from Solomon to announce the dedication of his new temple. It was 960 B. C., the same year, as I've said, of my son's birth. Zer has asked if she might describe what happened, so I will leave those details to her, as well. Suffice it for me to say that I regard the ugly circumstance of my death as providence, a divine setting of the stage for my son's eventual rebellion from Jerusalem and the House of David, and for his forsaking of the temple whose dedication played a role in my untimely death. I suspect that my being killed before he was born, and in the name of Solomon's Temple, played a deeply psychological role in guiding the decisions made by my son as king of Israel, walling off his nation from the building connected to his father's death. Your pyscho-analysts would surely have a field day with that one, would they not?

I deeply regret that I did not live to greet my son at Zer's side, never laying eyes on the boy destined for such greatness that would carry my name through the ages. As you can tell, I'm very proud of him, though from what you may have read in the history of your sacred pages you might wonder how a father could be proud of one whom history labels a scoundrel, an enemy of God. As Greg said in his opening monologue, let it not be forgotten that virtually every king following my son to the throne was described with a similar moniker, a variation of *"he did evil in the sight of the LORD, not turning away from the sins of Jeroboam ben Nebat, which he caused Israel to sin."* It is in that context, and that context only, that my name, Nebat, lives.

How could I be proud of a son like that, you ask? I'll tell you how, using a term with which I know you're familiar. Fake News! The official history of Israel, influenced by southern prophets, Jeroboam-haters all, intentionally skews the record to slander my son.

As a young builder possessing obvious genius, he was chosen by Solomon to lead in the most important real estate deals of the kingdom.

Greg is right, you may think of that, his entrance into government work, as an official in Solomon's Department of Labor. He would never have made it to that level of influence and power had he not been expert in the art of the deal, if you know what I mean.

But it wasn't my son's wheeling and dealing that turned him from being an official within Solomon's government to being his chief adversary. No, but that masterpiece of a deal was God's doing, Adonai's sovereign design. It was, in fact, the very prophet seated across from me at this table who chased down my son on a road outside Jerusalem to tell him that God had chosen him, my son, Jeroboam ben Nebat, to be king.

Were word of such whispered sedition to reach the ear of King Solomon, whether by spying or by leaking (you may be sure that we had both!), you can imagine the danger in which my son would be placed. And, in fact, the report of my son's treason did reach Solomon, which you have heard. I will leave it to my son to say more of his flight to Pharaoh for asylum, and of his return two years later to establish a new kingdom of Israel. It's a fascinating story to hear, and you will hear it tonight without all the Fake News that has, up until this moment, informed everything you may have thought you knew about Jeroboam ben Nebat. Tonight, prepare yourselves, for you will unlearn much of what you have learned.

How, you ask, could the Establishment media so effectively malign my son that Bible students 3,000 years later would still think of him as an arch villain? There's a simple answer to that question, and it is this. The winning side writes the history. Every student of history in search of truth must surely take into account that the history they read, of any time and of any era, has been written by the winning side. No historian can separate themselves entirely from their bias. It's impossible.

In the case of Judah and Israel, the only question as to which history would be read by coming generations was which kingdom would outlast the other, the winners able to edit out any writings with contrary views, expunging them completely out of the narrative. Jerusalem, the center of the Judahite dynasty of the House of David, lasted for over a century longer than Israel. That's why what you think you know about my son, Jeroboam ben Nebat, is Fake News. It's as simple as that. One hundred and forty years is plenty of time to shape the narrative.

Because Judah outlasted Ephraim, theirs is the voice you hear, a slanted verdict that ben Nebat led Israel to sin by leading the tribes in a commonsense real estate project in two of his cities on his northern and southern border, Dan in the north and Bethel in the south. In your day of Trump's Wall-talk, you may think of those cities as *Jeroboam's Wall*. The prophets condemned my son's wall as his way to siphon off the glory of the nation's faith from its epicenter, Jerusalem, in much the same way critics today speak of *Trump's Wall* as tarnishing the glory of the Statue of Liberty, the epicenter of hope for immigrants coming to America.

Those altars at Dan and, especially, at Bethel, Jeroboam's "Wall," became his unpardonable sin. What my son was actually doing, though, was re-establishing the holy places that our northern tribes had known for generations prior to King Solomon's new temple. Dan and Bethel? These were merely the holy cities which our older men and women and their ancestors had known as sacred prior to Solomon's temple.

Dan and Bethel was a proclamation of Jeroboam's MIGA, just like Trump's MAGA. With Dan and Bethel my son was saying, "*Make Israel Great Again!*"

Truth be told, I suspect Ahijah's real beef with my son, the reason he flipped, wasn't that he was angry that Jeroboam turned his back on Jerusalem as much as that my son didn't make his city, Shiloh, one of the new pilgrimage sites. That would have brought a lot of tourist dollars into Shiloh had my son chosen it for his southern wall instead of Bethel. I'm just sayin'.

So, yes, you'll understand if I describe the biblical record of my son's life as Fake News. When the kingdom my son founded fell, 200 years later in 721 B. C., there was no one to offer any counter-punch when his reputation was maligned. Southern historians were free to declare that the northern kingdom had been doomed from the start. Imagine! A nation enduring two centuries and ruled by nearly twenty kings after my son joined me in 'eretz ha-kadosh was doomed from the start? I confess I wonder how Israel's history would have been written had the reverse been true, had Ephraim outlasted Judah, allowing our northern scribes to be the framers of Hebrew history. A very different story it would have been, I assure you! David may have retained some glory, but not his son, Solomon. Our historians would have told the truth about the pain he brought to his people, such pain that led them to place a crown on my son's head.

But we'll never know, will we? No we won't, because Jerusalem, in fact, endured nearly 140 years longer than Ephraim, three full generations. Those years, from 721 B. C. to 586 B. C., the year Solomon's temple was destroyed by Nebuchadnezzar, gave ample time for historians in Judah to telescope all of Israel's problems, even its ultimate fall, back onto Israel's first king, Jeroboam ben Nebat. You were right, Greg, it's the equivalent of saying "Blame it on George!"

My friends, don't trust everything your media says, everything historians write. It's naïve to think news is ever offered without opinion, without slant. I think Emily Dickinson's line, "*Tell the truth, but tell it slant,*" must be the guiding principle for journalists, ancient and modern, experts at telling just enough truth so that their bias is not so obvious, their lies hidden.

I close by saying again, thank you for inviting us today to join you on *The Five*, our opportunity to set the record straight. Tonight you'll hear a truth which has taken 3,000 years gradually to emerge. That's the conclusion of Emily's poem, by the way, "*the truth must dazzle gradually, or every man be blind.*" It excites me that *The Five* is giving us the opportunity to tell the truth. And, who knows? Perhaps the truth will dazzle you.

Here's the truth. Blaming my son for Israel's fall 200 years after his death is surely one of the most egregious examples of Fake News in Hebrew history, maybe in all of human history. It's deranged. I've watched closely how your biblical scholars have treated my son through the years. My least favorite is a German word labeling my son as *Israel's Unheilsherrsher*, meaning, *The Unholy King*.

That's who my son was, if you believe the *Fake News*. *Unheilsherrscher*! I'm surprised they haven't yet used the word to tag

Donald Trump as *America's Unheilsherrscher*, the *Unholy King*. I suspect they'll use it now, my gift to them.

CHAPTER THREE

Zeruah, the mother of Jeroboam

———

Dana: As you can see, we have today an unusual and exciting edition of *The Five*. You've just heard from King Jeroboam's father, Nebat. Thank you, sir, for taking the lead in telling the fascinating story of your family and your country. Seated with me is Nebat's wife, Zeruah. We've heard a father's perspective, and I can't wait to hear what you have to say from a mother's perspective. Welcome.

Zeruah: *Toda raba*, Dana, thank you very much. My esteemed husband, in characteristic modesty, did not tell you what a wonderful man he truly was. Though taken from us far too young, Nebat was already highly regarded by the elders in our village of Zeredah, called to "*sit in its gates*," our way of describing community leaders who judged all matters arising within the village.

It was not long after I became pregnant that Nebat was first asked to sit in the gates of Zeredah. He rushed home to tell me of the honor extended to him by our village elders and I'll never forget his joy as he turned that honor to me, quoting parts of the poem you know as Proverbs 31: "*A virtuous woman, who can find? Her worth is far above that of rubies. Her husband is known in the gates, sitting with the elders of the land. Her children will rise up and call her blessed, her husband also, and he will praise her.*"

Elation filled both of us as we held each other that night, he placing his hand on my belly as if to draw ben Nebat into our joy. We dreamed together of how the child in my womb would one day rise up and call me blessed.

Jeroboam: And I do, mother. You are blessed, indeed!

Zeruah: Thank you, my son. I have felt your blessing and am proud of how your life honored both your father and our beloved tribe of Ephraim.

Dana, I could tell you so much more about this good man and wonderful husband, Nebat. He has a story too, you know, and I'm thankful to have shared it with him, however briefly. But you've invited us this evening to hear, not about Nebat, but about ben Nebat, so I will come to the point.

My husband mentioned the story of my name, and perhaps I should begin with that, another example of Fake News. In the chronicles of the kings of Israel and Judah the *ima*, the mother of Jeroboam ben Nebat, is Zeruah. That's how history knows me, and how you have introduced me. Let's change that now since, thankfully, that's not how my family and community knew me. I assure you, no one called me by that odious name, which in Hebrew means *"leprous."* My parents would never have given me such a name. It was Judah's historians from the south, of course, who gave me that name, saying what they thought of the mother of their adversary.

It's worse in the Septuagint, by the way, the Hebrew text translated into Greek nearly 1,000 years after I lived. There my name became Sarira. I rather like Sarira, but I don't like it that the text then openly calls me a whore, a vilification directed not at me, of course, but at my son.

In truth, the bastardization of my name retained only its first syllable, Zer, exactly what Nebat called me a moment ago. In fact, he called me Zer from the time we were children in our village of Zeredah. Since our town had the same first syllable as my name, he sometimes teased me, calling me *"Zer from Zer."* The Hebrew prefix meaning *"from"* begins with the "m" sound, so occasionally he called me *Zer-m-Zer.* It had a sing-song quality, and made me laugh.

My birth name was, in fact, Zerlinda, meaning *"Beautiful Dawn."* I was born, my ima and abba said, as a most beautiful dawn was giving birth to *yom hadesh*, a new day. It was twilight, dawn's shimmering rays breaking through night's darkness. Abba told me that the moment of twilight – at both ends of the day, dawn and dusk -- is the threshold moment when light and dark embrace and all things are possible. Yes, at dusk, as well as at dawn, all things are possible.

Abba loved to tell me how his first kiss upon my cheeks was just at that moment when light and dark kissed. I think that thought gave him a cosmic sense of providence, that God in his sovereignty had joined with nature to signal something very special in store for my life, that my birth signaled a new beginning. I suppose every father thinks the same at the birth of their child, no matter the hour, but my father was right about the amazing new beginning I would bring to Ephraim. I was destined for something special indeed, something that would change Israel and the world forever, since it was destined that I would give birth to ben Nebat.

My son was also born at twilight, but not at dawn. He was born at day's opposite end, at dusk. How I wish Nebat had been there to kiss his soft cheeks, just as my abba once kissed me but, as he told you, he was four months dead.

Nebat died on a hot summer day when the soldiers from Jerusalem arrived in Zeredah to inform us that we, joining all of Solomon's kingdom, were to observe a special festival in the seventh month of Ethanim, the month which came to be known later as Tishrei. Tishrei is the month of Sukkoth, the Feast of Tabernacles which, in your calendars, falls in September or October.

The soldiers message was that the fourteen day dedication of Solomon's Temple was to begin on the 8th day of Ethanim, still four months away. King Solomon, calling for a festive gathering in Jerusalem to join him on that first day of the dedication, had sent emissaries throughout the twelve tribes to invite delegations from each community's elders to represent their villages. I'm very sure that, had he lived, Nebat would have been present in Jerusalem to witness the Shekinah glory filling the temple.

In addition to the festivities in Jerusalem, each village throughout the tribes of Israel were to observe, simultaneously, a feast of thanksgiving for the completion of the temple. We, of course, knew that the temple had been virtually completed for nearly a year already. While the news announced that day came as no surprise, we were overjoyed that the time had come.

So exciting was this news that we didn't wait four months to celebrate. Most of the families of Zeredah gathered that very night, pouring the wine of celebration and dancing mightily. Not to celebrate the temple, you understand. No, but rather our joy was in hoping that all the families of Zeredah might now be reunited. Many families had been separated during the temple's construction, some of our youngest and most able men conscripted into a labor force for Solomon's building projects in a program called the *sebel*. My own brother, Abdiel, was one of these, taken from us over a year before in the *sebel*, so you can imagine how the news of the temple's dedication was exciting. Now we could pray with more vigor that our men would, at long last, come home.

You see, Solomon's policies were creating a forgotten class of people, these the very ones who would one day lift my son to the throne. When his time came, my son pledged to make their lives better, promising never to abuse the people as Solomon had abused them. Even before your republic form of government, you understand, the peoples' voice made a difference. I don't mean in the ballot box, the voice you Americans are blessed to have. You must thank God for that freedom and for the peaceful transfer of power. I mean to say that people everywhere and at all times have a voice, even under tyranny. When the situation grows dire, they find their voice. Always, they find their voice. Every tyrannical leader knows and fears this.

So, yes, Zereda drank and danced that night. Perhaps too much, because what happened that night cost my husband his life. About an hour after I had kissed Nebat and retired to rest in my chamber, fearing that the activity and excitement may harm my unborn child, I heard the laughter outside change to startled cries. Something had happened, but I had no idea until my mother burst into the room that what had happened would change my life forever.

Nebat, as I have said, was a proud Ephraimite. His favorite story, told so often around the campfires to the children of Zeredah, was how it was an Ephraimite, Joshua, who led the *bene yisrael*, the sons of Israel, over the Jordan River bearing the ark of the covenant, leading them on a march with seven revolutions around Jericho and blasting the shofar until its walls fell to the ground. Children in your day sing of Joshua fighting the battle of Jericho, how the "walls came a-tumblin' down." Nebat taught just such a song to the Ephraimite children of Zeredah, building pride in our Ephraimite heritage. I smile to think that, had my husband toted a bottle of Windex, he would have been the Ephraimite version of Gus, the family patriarch in that wonderful film, *My Big Fat Greek Wedding*, so proud of his heritage that he found a way to connect all English words to his beloved Greek. Nebat was like that. Anything that was important was somehow connected to his beloved Ephraim.

Nebat was proud that Ephraim was home to two of the most important cities of worship in Israel, Shiloh and Shechem. Ahijah, seated with us tonight, was no minor prophet. He was the prophet of

Shiloh, grandson of the more famous Eli, the *cohen gadol*, the "high priest" of Shiloh. It was Eli's prayer, perhaps you will remember, which blessed a barren woman named Hannah with a son whose name was Samuel, the same Samuel who changed Israel forever by giving us a king, making us a monarchy. Samuel discovered and anointed our first two kings, Saul the Benjaminite and David the Judahite.

It was my husband's pride in Ephraim that caused the scuffle which got out of hand, taking my husband's life. His boasting of Ephraim and its worship sites, especially Shiloh, was not received well by the soldiers from Jerusalem who, like Nebat and all of Zeredah, had consumed too much wine. I was told that the wine had loosened Nebat's tongue to say, unwisely, very unkind things about Jerusalem and her new temple, suggesting that he feared Solomon would force the Ephraimites to worship at this new temple, thereby forsaking their more ancient altars. I have no doubt that he said as much, liberated by drink not to think before he spoke.

They told me that what happened next was accidental. No swords drawn, nothing like that, no weapons. It was more like a bar fight ending in an accidental head injury. Struck by a soldier much stronger than he, Nebat fell to the ground, his head crashing against the sharp edge of rock. Israel has plenty of rocks.

You know, I think that this soldier even tried to apologize. How unusual! I could see it in his eyes, though, when I ran out to my husband. Keeping his distance, he saw I was with child. His eyes sought to offer consolation, I'm sure of it. No one, not even the soldiers, wished for a day of celebration to end like that. But it did, just like that, so that fatherless would be my son, Jeroboam ben Nebat. I suppose you could say that my husband, Nebat, died for the very idea which my son, ben Nebat, would one day lead our entire nation to accept, that Jerusalem and its Solomonic temple were not necessary to a true worship of God.

Grief and pregnancy don't mix well. I will admit my fear and anger in those last four months carrying my son. I was alone. Achingly alone.

O, but how ironic is God's timing! If my husband had died on the day Jerusalem sent word of the coming dedication of Solomon's Temple, ben Nebat was born on that very day, four months later! Not at dawn, as I have said, but at the other twilight moment, at dusk when the same light and dark embrace, marching in different directions, into darkness rather than light.

I confess that I wondered at his birth, already dark in soul because of Nebat's absence, what darkness ben Nebat may bring to Israel. A dark omen I took it to be, that the son of a woman born at dawn would be born at dusk. And how ominous that his birth was on the very day of the temple's dedication in the year you would call 960 B. C. Would my child, his first breath gulped as night swallowed the last rays of sunlight which shone upon the temple on its very first day, someday himself swallow the light shining upon Temple Mount in *Yerushalayim*?

I dreamed that night of Solomon's temple, its holy spaces filling with the Shekinah glory. In my dream our people, Ephraim, led by my son, turned their backs on the temple to kneel at altars over which roiled dark clouds, like those you saw churning down the streets of Manhattan when the Towers collapsed.

Little did I know then that my dusk-born, fatherless son would lead Ephraim to forsake Jerusalem and to kneel to the golden calves of Dan and Bethel. But there was a reason for that, which is his story to tell, and I think that my son is next to speak.

CHAPTER FOUR

King Jeroboam ben Nebat

———

Jesse: Wow, what a great set-up from your mother! My mother sometimes contributes to *The Five* with text messages scolding me for, occasionally, going too far. I wonder if that's what the mother of King Jeroboam has just said to her son? Did you go too far?

America, I can't wait to hear from our next guest, King Jeroboam ben Nebat, whose building of worship sites in Dan and Bethel, Jeroboam's Wall, earned him the title of *Unheilsherrscher, The Unholy King*. Your majesty, welcome! I can't wait to hear what you have to say.

Jeroboam: *Shalom*, Jesse, and *erev tov*, good evening. You must know that yours is a wonderful Hebrew name, Yishai, pointing to the bearer of that name as a *"gift."* I've watched you, and so you are, aptly named. You are a gift, a fantastic, beautiful person! I like you very much, as I know do all your citizens in Watter's World.

The biblical Jesse, by the way, was the father of King David, the grandson of Ruth and Boaz whose love story is told in the book of Ruth. It's my very favorite biblical story, in no small part because of Ruth's outsider status.

You see, despite what you've called -- correctly I might add – Jeroboam's Wall, I love immigrants. Ruth was the Bible's best-known immigrant, an ancestor of our King David and of your own Jesus of Nazareth. God's providence brought her in and made her name live forever.

While I was not a gentile outsider as was she, a Moabitess, I was in the political world a total outsider. That's why her story thrills me. It was God's plan to raise me to the throne so that I could help a forgotten people and give them a chance for a better life, a pathway to make their lives great again. The arrogant, selfish, ignorant policies of Solomon had diminished the quality of life throughout the tribes of Israel.

If I was *Unheilherrscher* it was only in the eyes of my enemies, not of my people. My policies enriched their lives, and they knew it. Like your president, I could have filled arenas with enthusiastic followers. It's not hard to understand why. The beautiful, incredible people of our northern tribes were being hurt by Solomon. I wondered sometimes how that man could possibly be thought of as the epitome of *hokmah*, our Hebrew word meaning "*wisdom.*"

I admit, though, he was a wonderful writer. If there had been Nobel prizes in our day, he surely would have won the prize for *Hokmah (Wisdom) Literature*, which in our day was as popular as your cinema blockbusters from Hollywood. It was our primary source, not only for education and enlightenment, but also for sheer entertainment. Which is fitting, since I regard Solomon as a joke.

Yes, he could write, I'll give him that. Literature was his forte, owning a prowess celebrated by all the Wisdom writers in the East in the same way your culture holds celebrities in awe. I've never understood, by the way, how mere actors' opinions are given such press. Why would people care what they think? They're actors, for God's sake, repeating words not their own, borrowing from the stories and glories of others.

I've sometimes wondered who would play me were my story ever to be taken up by Hollywood. I think that fellow who played Jesus in *The Passion of the Christ*, Jim Caviezel, would be my choice. I prefer, though, his role as *The Count of Monte Cristo*, which may say something about how much I would love to get back at my enemies in the press. It was they, enemies of the people, who damaged my reputation. Their lies lifted the reputation of the vile Solomon, whose cruel policies hurt the people so much that they revolted, raising me to the throne believing I could relieve and remove (or, should I say "repeal and replace"?) the burden Solomon had forced them to bear.

Still, no matter how excellently Mr. Caviezel might play the role of Jeroboam ben Nebat, his voice on political matters should amount to no more than any other person. He would have played me on the screen. He would not have been me.

Solomon too, in many ways, was a play-actor, the celebrity of his time as a writer of pretty proverbs, a champion of verse. In this he excelled. But when it came to leading the economy, Solomon had not a clue. Sad. Very sad!

A ruler should put in place such economic policies that might better the lives of his people. Solomon did not, obviously, for had he done so I would never have been made king. You would not know my name and I would not be on *The Ten* tonight. If my charismatic leadership fanned the flames of rebellion, you may be sure that it didn't light the match. Solomon's failed economic policies were sufficient for that. Without question, had Solomon been a wiser leader my name in the biblical record would have been a footnote merely, a servant of Solomon pretty good at the art of the deal and at building walls.

Solomon the Wise? *Solomon the Stupid* is more like it! I realize I sound now like your president, giving names to my political foes. Like him, I did love a good fight. I especially love it when Mr. Trump calls out the stupidity of previous administration whose deals gave away so much, whether actual hard cash as in the Iran deal, or in trade policies driving jobs into foreign markets and weakening prospects of economic growth at home. And why? All so that Mr. Obama could be venerated as wise on the global stage.

Or, wait. Am I talking about Solomon now? Hell, I can't tell! Like Obama, Solomon was all about his globalist ambitions. His reputation internationally is what mattered. I, on the other hand, was a nationalist. I wanted a better life for my people. Israel first. Not Israel only, mind you, but emphatically Israel first. Nationalism was my core, and it made me successful, just as it has for your president.

It's fascinating to me how liberals and globalists pride themselves in being social justice warriors. Solomon's PR machine sought to cast him in just that way, "woke" to the needs of the disadvantaged, concocting a story of two harlots fighting over one living baby. *"Bring a sword,"* he said, *"to cut the child in two, and let each have half!"* And THAT'S supposed to be an evidence of Solomon's woke wisdom, of his social justice? Give me a break! It was a mirage to make him appear wise, oozing with compassion and tender to social justice concerns.

Truth is, I, as a nationalist, was the true social justice warrior. I was the one who came to the rescue of families whose lives had been ruined by Solomon. I lifted them up, all of them together, every segment of society. His reputation for social justice was an illusion, just as is all that is offered by socialism and communism. As good as it looks, as much as it promises and pretends to care, it doesn't work well. Make no mistake, Solomon's policies were leading Israel toward becoming Venezuela.

If Solomon's words sounded intelligent and mine less so, less literary, then so be it. My words may not have been as eloquent, but they made more sense and contained more hope of actually bettering people's lives. What I offered the people is something pretty proverbs are powerless to provide. As Mr. Trump, I cared nothing for being "presidential," a paradigm which in practice lulls people to sleep.

When attacked, I hit back. My people in the northern ten tribes found that refreshing, just as conservative Americans are finding the rough edges of your president to be absolutely bracing. *"Finally! A politician with a backbone to speak his mind openly in defense of conservative principles! A president who speaks directly to us without the media, using common, even if sometimes vulgar, language."* The media despises him for that, even as they join with him in that, he drawing them into a fight on his turf. Yes, but his supporters love him for it, thinking, *"At last, a leader who will fight for us!"*

Well then, let me fight for my reputation after these 3000 years of lies from the Bible. Dan and Bethel, you ask? Why *Jeroboam's Wall?* Seems like that question is all I heard through 22 years on my throne and then for 200 more years, each successor on the throne pilloried for not reversing my Wall policy. There is more *Fake News* in the Bible on this topic, Jeroboam's Wall, than about anything else in all of biblical history. The media simply didn't get it, but the success of the policy is evident in the fact – the FACT – that no king after me, not ONE king who ruled for the next 200 years, tore down that wall. Why? Because it worked, that's why! Don't overanalyze this. It's really not at all complicated.

Jeroboam's Wall made us winners. It was the right policy, a strategic move fully supported by all my advisors. You've called it a "virtual" Wall, and that is true. In fact, some men, leaders from the tribes closest to my southern border, advising against my new worship centers, wishing for us to continue to make pilgrimage to *Yerushalayim* in order to appease the Establishment, called my Bethel shrine *ha-homa shel Yarobam*, the Wall of Jeroboam. Was it at first unpopular? Sure, but the truly great leaders are willing to do the unpopular thing for the long-term benefit of the nation. Trump gets that, which makes him a winner in my book. Interesting, is it not, that issues surrounding *ha-homa*, the Wall, are still headline news not only in America with Trump and the issue of immigration, but also in Israel with the issue of terrorism and, goodness, even on *The Walking Dead*, a show I much enjoyed, survivors of the zombie apocalypse searching for sanctuary, any solid wall that might protect them.

My Wall, though, wasn't about immigration or terrorism or zombies. My Wall was about creating and preserving our national identity. Which, when I think on that, isn't that the undergirding reason for Trump's Wall in the south and the wall of Israel along the West Bank? Immigration and terror may be the presenting issues, but both were national emergencies operating in the realm of preserving national identity. That's the reason for Jeroboam's Wall, and that's the reason for Trump's Wall.

So yes, I'm very proud that my very first act as a new king in Ephraim was the construction of those sites at our northern and southern borders. I built them as holy shrines, as pilgrimage destinations. I walled our nation in, north and south, not to keep illegals out, as Trump's Wall seeks to do, but to center our people's allegiance at home. My Wall was critical to our survival as a nation.

It was the commonest of common sense, purely rational thought (and that's a shout-out for you Mr. Wilkow – I LOVE your show!). I could not have kept my promises to my people without my Wall and, if I was anything, I was a leader determined to keep my promises. It was a difficult and controversial decision, but it paid off and kept our fledgling nation from downfall. Trust me, the nation of Israel would have collapsed in infancy without *ha-homa shel Yarobam*, which is why it was a national emergency.

It's all about contextualization, which makes me the liberal when you think about it. The context of our new nation demanded it, in the same way your Mainline Christian denominations have bowed to the context of the shifting mores of American cultural life on issues of human sexuality and same-sex marriage. You don't see the Southern Baptists doing that! Only liberal denominations dare be contextual, dare to change what has always been.

"Same gender marriage? Why not? The culture demands it and the Supreme Court of the land has endorsed it. Ancient teaching be damned. Tradition be damned. We must change with the culture." That's contextualization. That progressive. And, guess what? That's what Jeroboam's Wall was!

Do you see what I'm saying? I am tonight being compared to a conservative president of your country, but Jeroboam's Wall was anything but conservative. It was contextual. My act was the very definition of being progressive, liberalism at its best. I wonder, then, who is the real liberal here, today, in your country?

I made the tough choices, despite the people's lack of understanding why it must be done. Media condemnations had little impact on me. It was the right thing to do, pure and simple. Had I allowed pilgrimages to *Yerushalayim*, hearts would have turned to *Yerusalayim*, and to its king, *Low I. Q. Rehoboam*.

Well, look at me now! I've borrowed Trump's name for Maxine Waters, she whose rants deeply embarrass. That woman is an unwitting boon for the Republicans. I read a conservative writer recently who invoked an ancient Hebrew blessing upon her from the Book of Numbers. Of Maxine, after one of her especially dumb rants, he wrote, *"May the Lord bless her and keep her . . . in the news!"*

I felt exactly that way about *Low I. Q. Rehoboam!* The more my people thought of him and his lunatic pronouncements about thick little fingers and scorpion whippings, the more they loathed him. I could have pronounced the ancient Hebrew blessing over my rival in the same way. *"May the Lord bless you, Low I. Q. Rehoboam, and keep you . . . in the news!"*

Rehoboam combined weakness with ignorance, not listening to his wiser counselors. Just like Hillary! Hillary and her advisors didn't listen to Bill, either. His wisdom could have helped her win in 2016, but she ignored his warning that her campaign was overlooking the forgotten voters in those fly-over Rust Belt states that ultimately elected Trump. The Dems were too busy playing identity politics to listen to wise counsel. Hillary didn't listen. Rehoboam didn't listen. Peas of a pod!

Oh my, look what he's done to me, your President Trump! I like him so much I find myself looking for names to call my ancient opponents! Before I go further, though, may I get serious for a moment to say something about my own name?

You should know that it's not a given that history would know me as Jeroboam ben Nebat. Does history think of David as David ben Jesse, or Solomon as Solomon ben David? No, and there is a reason, though not, perhaps, what you're thinking. Obviously, Hebrew history has been unkind to me. I own arch-villain status, something like being compared to Hitler, an aspersion cast by the Left today, I've noticed, on anyone who disagrees with them. But I digress. What I'm saying is that nowadays those perpetrating great evil are often known by their full names: John Wilkes Booth, Lee Harvey Oswald, John Wayne Gacy. Perhaps you're thinking Hebrew history did the same to me, thus, Jeroboam ben Nebat, my full name, as a way to emphasize how wicked I was?

No. While Fake News historians may have given my mother a hideous name, they had nothing to do with my name. That was my doing. Having never had the opportunity to know my father I decided, early in life, long before I rose in the ranks as one of Solomon's chief builders, to carry my abba with me in all that God might lead me to accomplish. As a very young man I let it be known that my name was not merely Jeroboam, but Jeroboam ben Nebat, intending that my father, unknown to me, would be known to the world. This would be my gift to my abba, who died defending our ancient tribal customs against Solomon's intent to diminish Ephraim by forcing pilgrimage to his temple in Yerushalayim.

My life may have assured his place in history, but you should know that his memory, still fresh in my village when I was a child, shaped me. Fatherless, I did not lack in father figures. Our community elders, perhaps out of pity but, in time, observing my raw gifts and wishing to shape them, were eager to provide guidance. Or, I suppose it's possible that they just wanted an excuse to be close to my widowed mother, she so blessed with beauty in body and soul.

My ima told me many times about my birth at dusk on the day Solomon's Temple was dedicated, and of her dream, her nightmare, that my birth might someday diminish the glory of that temple in *Yerushalayim*. Solomon the Dawn. I the Dusk. Her dream was always with me.

If we had been English-speakers back then, I would have created a crest from two Ds facing each other and interlocking, symbolizing *Dawn* and *Dusk*. The overlap of the two facing Ds would create an almond-shape right in the middle known as the *mandorla*, the Italian word for almond. That overlap represents a threshold from one D to the other D, from *Dawn* to *Dusk*. I was that threshold. In Jewish history it was I who sat in the mandorla, the dusk of Solomon's glory followed by the dawn of a new nation conceived to alleviate the agony of the people suffering under Solomon's government.

What a great bulla, or seal, that would have made for marking my official documents. I would have put that symbol throughout my palace, commanding my administration to seal all official documents with it, a declaration that my moment in Israel's history was a threshold into something new. What was yesterday and at my very birth a new *Dawn*, Solomon's temple, had now met its *Dusk* in Jeroboam's two altars, my Walls in the north and the south, Dan and Bethel. And do you see how the outer edges of the interlocking D's create solid walls, as if in the north and the south? We were a nation within a nation, Israel within Israel. What a beautiful crest it would have been, and meaningful. Ah, but where was English when I needed it?

Did you realize, by the way, that your own Washington Monument in D. C. is placed squarely in the same geometric figure of the mandorla? It's true. The phallic symbol of the Washington Monument, as is clearly seen from the air, is placed in the pavement perfectly in the middle of mandorla. It should be no wonder. I was the Washington of my time, bringing the nation through an important moment in our history. Or, perhaps I would be more accurate to say that George Washington was the Jeroboam of his time, leading the colonies out of the old circle of the British Empire and crossing the mandorla, as surely as he crossed the Delaware, into the new circle of the United States of America.

Perhaps even more fascinating as a comparison is that just as in my kingdom the more volatile border, the place where our vulnerability was dangerously exposed and therefore needing protection, was the southern border.

Jesse, any *Dusk* will, soon enough, become the *Dawn* of something new. If I was *Dusk* for Solomon and his temple, I was also the *Dawn* of a new day. Your English poet T. S. Eliot said it concisely, "In my end is my beginning," and I, Jeroboam ben Nebat, was Israel's new beginning.

My mother's dream planted in me the idea that I was destined for work in Solomon's building projects, and I don't mean as a conscripted laborer, such as my Uncle Abdiel. No, but I determined to learn all I could about architecture and engineering. Mother educated me as best she could, with the help of Zeredah's elders, and I grew rapidly in knowledge and ability. As you have heard already this evening, by God's sovereign providence Solomon noticed me, so that I rose in the ranks until at last he named me Under Secretary of the Department of Labor!

My ima was as proud of me when she heard the news of Solomon's appointment as she was fearful that her dream would come to pass. Directing the labor force from the northern tribes, I had a close-up view of the pain our families endured in order to support Solomon's extravagances. I wanted to help them, to *Make Israel Great Again*, though MIGA, somehow, doesn't look as good on caps as MAGA, lacking somewhat in symmetry. I jest, of course, as I put on my blue MIGA hat, but isn't the return to past glory the theme of every political outsider's ambition?

I'm not suggesting that Israel had lost all its glory under Solomon. Solomon's temple in Jerusalem, exactly to the day as old as I, was indeed glorious. Israel shone bright as Solomon's glory spread throughout the kingdoms to the east and west, north and south. Heads of state flocked to see his glory. Best known to you, no doubt, is the Queen of Sheba. She was left breathless, her heart fluttering (and I mean that in the most literal and sensual of ways) at his displays of wisdom and wealth.

Still, as much as Solomon was revered, the foundations of his administration were crumbling. Not, as the prophets maintained, because of his dalliances with other cultures and gods, our prophets soundly condemning his embrace of multi-culturalism. Solomon could have weathered prophetic condemnations. What he could not escape was the people's reaction to the harm being done by his domestic economic policy. That brought him down. *"It's the Economy Stupid!"* was my phrase long before it was Carville's! That message brought me to the throne of Israel.

I am, as you can clearly see, a careful of observer of American politics, and not without opinion. Fully aware I am that your last president, Obama, though lauded globally -- a Nobel Prize winner, no less! -- presided over a time of sluggish economic growth through such regulation and taxation that drove jobs away. He should have built my kind of wall, a wall to keep businesses from relocating outside the borders of the country. The only possible result of his policies would be increasing polarization at home, all while being lauded as *Obama the Wise* on the global stage, just like Solomon. Such "Wise Ones" unwittingly set the stage for another. I speak now of both Solomon and Obama, twin

Wise Ones; and of both Jeroboam and Trump, the unexpected result of their true lack of wisdom.

Working in Solomon's administration as head of the *sebel*, which is to say, the conscripted labor force, I couldn't get my mother's dream out of my head. He the Dawn. I the Dusk. I don't say her dream plagued me. No. It thrilled me! If I am the Dusk, I thought, I might also be the Dawn, leading the people to step across the mandorla threshold into a new day. Like the Washington Monument, I would rise from the mandorla, gloriously.

I was pondering my mother's dream as I worked on the Millo in Jerusalem, one of the great renovation projects of Solomon in ʿir David (the City of David). The Millo was the fill, the wall, that supported the royal palace and was perhaps my grandest architectural accomplishment. I was thrilled when your archaeologist Kathleen Kenyon first discovered the massive stepped stone structure in the 1960s. What memories flooded back as I saw my Millo being unearthed!

One day, while taking a break from the construction site and walking alone, I was approached by a strange looking man. He posed no danger, that was clear, but what an odd man he was, a holy man, the very Ahijah of Shiloh who joins us today on *The Ten*. What he did was even stranger than how he looked. Without speaking, he removed his cloak, a new garment, and began to rip it up. He said nothing until he had counted twelve pieces. Then, holding two back as if not to relinquish them, he handed me all the rest, forcing me to take them. All ten of them.

At last he spoke, *"Take ten pieces for yourself, for the LORD, the God of Israel says, 'I will tear away the kingdom from Solomon's grasp and will give you ten of the tribes. One tribe shall remain for him for the sake of David, my servant, and of Jerusalem, the city I have chosen out of all the tribes of Israel. The ten I will give you because he has forsaken me and has worshiped Astarte, goddess of the Sidonians.'"* After that, he continued to rattle off even more unfaithful allegiances of Solomon. They would bore you, so I'll skip over his offenses.

I can only guess that Solomon had spies following me, or the prophet, or both. Of course he would have spies throughout his administration on all potential political foes, just as Obama's FBI and DOJ surely had on candidate Trump. Corrupt to the core is the Deep State, do not doubt me on that point! There's your real collusion, by the way. Make no mistake, the Deep State does not slumber nor sleep, and is never drowsy.

Fortunately, I became aware of Solomon's suspicions of my disloyalty and learned of his plan to have me killed. I had my own spies, you may be sure of that.

My only option was to flee, despite several of my key supporters urging me to stand my ground, to start the revolt. But I knew we weren't strong enough to challenge Solomon so, after disappointing them by saying, "We'll see what happens," I departed for Egypt. I realize the Jewish-Roman historian Josephus records that I gathered three hundred chariots to begin the revolt. Ha! Fake News! That surprises me, honestly, because Josephus is generally accurate.

No, in fact the revolt I had dreamed of since Ahijah's prophecy never got off the ground, so in this case the biblical record is accurate when it ignores it completely. I have no idea where Josephus got the idea that I could amass three hundred chariots. I suppose he just made it up. Believe me, there was no "there" there! Solomon's spies discovered me before I could devise any plan other than to escape. Three hundred chariots? Hell, I couldn't have amassed three! I wasn't ready. Running was my only option.

Pharaoh Shishak, I knew, was always on the lookout for influential friends from neighboring kingdoms. In my case, collusion was a reality forced upon me by the actions of my political adversary. I saw in Shishak a powerful potential friend who might, in some future moment, be helpful. He, of course, saw the same in me, a former member of Solomon's cabinet.

I was young, 28 years old. My stay in Egypt lasted only two years, but in that time Pharaoh and I became close, building an alliance.

We knew Solomon's days were numbered. In those days, of course, royalty was what mattered, not elections, and pharaoh gave me the royal credentials I needed by offering the hand of the beautiful Ano, his daughter.

Now, before any of your scholar viewers call in to tell me I must not know who I married, let me assure you I do. I'm fully aware that the Septuagint caused confusion by speaking of Ano as both pharaoh's daughter and as his sister-in-law, the older sister of his wife. The text is oddly worded in a way that leans toward seeing Ano as his sister-in-law, while allowing the possibility that she was his princess daughter. I'm mystified by that mistake. I knew his sister-in-law and I'll tell you now, I would never have married her. Never! Very plain, and very – O, my God -- very old!

Princess Ano was his daughter, believe me. Gorgeous, as you see her today, and incredibly smart. I have no idea how the "Pharaoh's sister-in-law" thing ever got started in textual commentary.

Well, actually, that's not true. I know exactly what the problem was. Just before I am introduced in 1 Kings 11:26, the narrative tells of Hadad the Edomite, a man who rebelled against Solomon in an earlier part of his reign, when I was but a boy. The biblical text clearly tells of pharaoh's harboring him, just as he did me, and is explicit in saying that pharaoh gave to Hadad his sister-in-law in marriage, the older sister of Queen Tahpenes.

In this the Bible is correct. But note that the Hebrew text never says of my wife that she was pharaoh's sister-in-law. That is only in the Septuagint, not the Bible. Bottom line is that the idea that my wife was

Pharaoh's sister-in-law rather than his daughter is a conflation of those two biblical texts, an understandable, if unfortunate, mix up. Perhaps the translator who first penned such a thought had been drinking too much, his mistake opening the door for that error to enter the stream of textual transmission.

Speaking of drinking, you should know that, like your president, I never touched a drop. It's not that I took a Nazarite vow of abstinence or anything like that. No, but for whatever reason alcohol never had any appeal for me, never crossing these lips, something much more unusual in my day than in the present day. Almost unheard of, in fact.

I smile to remember what a problem that caused for me with Pharaoh Shishak on the day of my wedding to his daughter. My new father-in-law expected me to join him in celebration by imbibing the highest quality imported wine, interpreting my abstinence as a lack of enthusiasm bordering on disrespect. Pharaoh loved his beer, but on this occasion, wine was flowing. Beer, known as *heqet* in Egyptian, was a staple drink for all classes of people. The Egyptians had a red wine called *shedeh*, but from what I hear it wasn't worth drinking. Good wine was more expensive and reserved for the wealthy, imported from the Levant in the north, near my home in the Galilee. Wine in Egypt was inferior due to the extremely hot and dry conditions of Egypt's climate. Still, even though the Galilean wine at my wedding would have reminded me of home, I abstained.

Oh, but Pharaoh did love his beer. Beer was very popular and almost everyone drank it for health reasons. It's no wonder your archaeologists have found beer recipes in the hieroglyphics and depictions on the walls of tombs as to how it was made. Still, I refused, despite the risk to my health due to unclean water. I was under no obligation not to drink, you understand, it was just a personal decision, despite knowing how unhealthy it could be for me. But, remember, my father had died because wine has loosened his lips to say ill-advised things. I wanted always to be in control of my emotions, and thus of my tongue.

Still, even drinking the water, I survived and thrived. When Solomon died two years later, I now 30 years old in 930 B. C., the ten tribes sent word for me to help them fashion an appeal to *Low I. Q. Rehoboam*, he having been already crowned king. I departed immediately and led the delegation respectfully to ask King Rehoboam to lighten the burden his father's economic policies had placed upon the people. He asked for three days to ponder his response.

That's when *Low I. Q. Rehoboam* came close to doing something wise, first seeking counsel from his older advisors, those who had served alongside his father. They said, *"If you will be a servant to this people today and serve them, they will be your servants forever."* Ah, the wisdom of age and experience!

His younger advisors, though, disagreed, counseling him to assert power. And so he did, vainly boasting in the re-assembled conclave, *"My little finger* (which, make no mistake, was a euphemism for a different bodily protuberance) *is thicker than my father's loins. I will add to your yoke, and discipline you not with whips, but with scorpions."* Sad! Very sad! Rehoboam spoke of his little finger, but this was his middle finger raised to all of Israel.

Like his father before him, Rehoboam despised the people as deplorables, which is why he was determined not to negotiate. He offered us only more of the same, a promise to continue the failed globalist policies of his father. Solomon, and now his son, forced the people to eat a diet of globaloney. I was the only one willing to call his hand, to voice the truth others feared speak. This forced *Low I. Q. Rehoboam* to show his hand clearly, making our decision easy. The allegiance of Ephraim, along with the coalition of ten tribes, was forever departed from the House of David.

Rehoboam thought his stern response to our demands would create fear among our leadership, fraying our new alliance to the point that I would be forced to flee back to pharaoh. He was wrong. His harsh statement, rather than creating fear, radicalized even the timid among my followers. He was playing right into my hands.

Seeing the situation spinning out of control, he sent a representative from his Department of Labor to soothe our anger, perhaps even to make a few minor concessions. That's the moment things turned violent. This man, Adoram, a former friend of mine who had worked under my direct supervision when I headed Solomon's Department of Labor, was killed. I didn't condone that violence, especially not aimed at such a good man as Adoram who was merely following his king's orders. I grieved for his wife and children, whom I knew. But there was no turning back now, as things were spinning out of control. With this unexpected assassination the tables were turned. Shechem was our territory now, and dangerous. The king had not expected that and was not ready. Now it was Rehoboam's turn to run, his chariot rushing him back to Jerusalem.

Honestly, it puzzled me why Rehoboam didn't fight harder to avoid the dissolution of the United Kingdom ruled by his father Solomon and grandfather David, and Saul the Benjaminite before them. So what that one of his prophets, Shemaiah, delivered to him a so-called "word" from the LORD to cease and desist because *this thing is from me?* I would have ignored such advice. I never would have quit so easily and, truth be told, we weren't at all as prepared for a fight as he might have thought we were. Fragile we surely were in this moment of our beginning, but he let that moment pass. While I suspect that a battle at that moment would have been devastating for us, Rehoboam heeded his advisor prophet and ordered his militia to stay home. So, just like that, it was all over.

What a poor leader Rehoboam was, listening to his advisors only when they offered stupidity, this the second time in the space of only a few days when his ears were open to mindless inanity. The sun was setting over the House of David, and I enjoyed the view from my new capitol. The reawakened sun would now rise over Israel and over ben Nebat, her new king.

The people were already beginning to feel the warmth of that sunrise when, that very day, I led them in the chant I had written:

What share do we have in David?
We have no inheritance in the son of Jesse.
To your tents, O Israel!

49

Look now to your own house, O David!

Not nearly as well written, I know, as the pretty proverbs of Solomon. Still, it stated the case clearly and got the job done. I was living up to the meaning of my Hebrew name, "*May the people be great.*" Mine was a clarion call for division, a nationalist message of radical change not unlike the 2016 election of a president sent to Washington as a force of disruption, promising to drain the swamp. In both cases, 3,000 years separated, the people were saying, "*Enough! We will not abide more of the same policies that have weakened us and divided us.*"

The ten tribes, now broken away from Jerusalem, gathered in a raucous assembly and there made me king over all of Israel with the exception of the tribe of Judah. I would say it was the largest gathering for an inauguration ever, but that line's already been used, if you know what I mean. I was 30 years old, the same age as David when he, the grandfather of my adversary, had been made king over Israel.

If my name, "*May the people be great,*" had been my campaign slogan, now the image of a new day dawning would become the leitmotif of my government. There were, of course, challenges. My being made king wasn't a unanimous opinion by all the elders of the tribes. There were those who feared my leadership would risk too much. It's hard to give up what is old, even when the old is repressive. That's why the Hebrews under Moses in the wilderness ached for Egypt, yearning to return to the prison walls of an earlier pharaoh than my friend, Shishak. At least in Egypt they had food, onions and, of course, beer. So much beer! None of that in the wilderness, where they were dependent on God's provision.

Some tribal leaders thought I was taking them into the wilderness, so it's no wonder that some wanted to go backward instead of forward. My response was basically what Mr. Trump, as a candidate, said to minority groups. "*What have you got to lose?*" I said. "*The establishment, the House of David, has made your lives miserable, especially Solomon in his foolish pursuit of global praise, and at your expense. His policies are not bettering your lives, which should be the true function of government. You can't deny this. Now his son promises more of the same. So I ask you, What the hell have you got to lose?*"

In that assembly I discovered my love for rallies. I was good at it and found that the charge I got from the electricity was addictive. "*What have you got to lose?*" connected with the people as they enthusiastically embraced me as their new king.

I told them in my speech that Solomon's glory on the worldwide stage, as exemplified in the Queen of Sheba story, a globaloney sandwich if ever there was one (which I tasted again when Obama won the Nobel Peace Prize), had been accomplished on their backs, by his ignoring his people's despair. One of my favorite lines was to remind them how Solomon himself wrote of the people's despair in a collection of poems which later became known as Ecclesiastes, the supposedly wise words of *Qoheleth* (*The Teacher*).

What was Solomon teaching them, I asked, but that the people should simply accept that life is hard and won't get better? Ecclesiastes is a "*Those jobs are not coming back!*" book, if you catch my drift.

Like your Obama, our Solomon was a soothing philosopher, but not a great leader of the economy. When your policies are hurting people, a good skill to have is to speak smoothly, something Solomon possessed in abundance, as does Obama. The Hebrew words Solomon wrote enter the ear with an oddly hypnotic quality, as if attempting to make drowsy the people: "*Hevel hevelim, ha-col hevel.*" Even in English those words enter the ear with an alliterative, sing-song quality, "*Vanity of vanities, all is vanity,*" followed by the question, "*What is life but a chasing after the wind?*"

Those at my rallies cheered wildly as I told them that *Solomon the Stupid* had used these words as a narcotic to numb the melancholy of those for whom his policies were creating misery. Solomon's message was obvious. "*Life can't get any better so, live with it!*"

As one who joined the Trump Train long ago, I couldn't help but remember my speech at Shechem when I heard Obama tell the people who had lost their jobs in certain manufacturing sectors, "*Those jobs are gone, and they're not coming back.*" In other words, "*get used to it!*"

The people in my day, and in your own, weren't willing to accept that. They wanted more, and if I am anything, I'm all about more. I told them we would be winning so much they would get tired of winning. And so we did. We won and we won and we won, though the prophets would not have admitted it any more than your Destroy Trump media, as that wonderful Mr. Hannity calls it, is willing to herald your president's many accomplishments.

Here's the sum of my story. I was a pragmatic leader. The Wall, as you have called it, my altars at Dan and Bethel, was not radical at all, but a commonsense contextualization made necessary by the situation.

I needed to secure the long-term allegiance of the people, and the wall was the only way to ensure that.

Was I condemned for it by the political class? You bet, and that didn't bother me a bit. All my acts were condemned by the prophets of the House of David, remember? I was *Doomed from the Start*. It's frustrating when your successes are overlooked, never mentioned by the media class with influence among the people. All they could talk about was my Wall, and all of that negative, never seeing the necessity caused by the emergency. Still, in such a climate of prophetic fury one becomes inured to media condemnations. Who cares what they write? The people know better, they see through the *Fake News*.

Finally, let me say how ironic it is for me that, even now, 3,000 years later, the decision to move your embassy to Jerusalem was met with such scorn by your media. It was the right thing to do, pure and simple. All recent presidents knew it was the right thing, promising it would be done. It wasn't, though, not until Mr. Trump delivered on that promise, doing what common sense demanded. It took a businessman, you see, to overrule political caution and do the right thing. That's what the people voted for in Trump, and that's what the people wanted when they placed a crown on my head so long ago.

But I shall pass the baton now to my prophet friend, Ahijah, who will agree, I think, with my last point, if with nothing else, he being such a lover of *Yerushalayim shel zahav* (*Jerusalem of Gold*).

CHAPTER FIVE

Ahijah, the prophet of Shiloh

———

Juan Williams: Well, I must add to the parallels we've seen tonight between King Jeroboam and President Trump that both own a tartness of tongue. I can only imagine, King Jeroboam, what you could have done had you had a Twitter account.

What an amazing story our audience is hearing tonight, and with much more to come. My guest at our table of ten is Ahijah, the prophet of Shiloh who will, no doubt, offer a different view on this 3000-year-old biblical story.

I'm fascinated by what I've read of my special guest tonight, Ahijah the prophet. I hadn't realized that many Jews today regard him as somewhat of a Yoda figure in Star Wars. He is reputed to be a Master of Secret Lore, and in Hasidic legend he came back in the 18th century to be the mystical teacher of Ba'al Shem Tov, the founder of Kabbalistic, mystical thought in Judaism. I can't wait to hear the prophet's views of the Jeroboam story. Welcome, sir, to *The Ten.*

Ahijah: *Toda raba*, Juan, "*thank you very much.*" Listening patiently to your previous guests, I'm happy at last to speak and set the record straight. That's what prophets do, right? We set the record straight, no matter whom it may upset. It's a tough job being a prophet, but somebody's got to do it. Am I right?

I'll begin with this, that what Nebat and his son have condemned as Fake News on the basis that it was written by southern historians and slanted toward Jerusalem, was not fake at all. Here's the truth, that God's blessing rested upon Jerusalem and its temple, not upon Jeroboam's altars at Dan and Bethel. I would say the same had he set up his altar in my own Shiloh, despite Nebat's vile assertion that my turning against his son had anything to do with jealousy on my part.

The great 12th century Jewish scholar Maimonides said it perfectly, that every human person has a choice to be righteous as was Moses, or to be evil, as Jeroboam. No doubt there are many listening tonight who, knowing their biblical history, have been astonished by Jeroboam's defense of his actions while leveling against the Bible charges of Fake News. I'm happy to be on this panel as a guide to any who may be perplexed by the claims made here tonight by the king and his family.

Nebat has said that the written history of the Bible is slanted toward Jerusalem. Well, of course our written history is slanted toward Jerusalem. How could it be otherwise, God having chosen Jerusalem as his holy city? Divine purpose is why Judah survived beyond Israel, and if southern prophets became the primary tellers of that history, God willed it to be so.

Jeroboam had his chance and blew it when he turned his back on God's city, *Yerushalayim*. "*As the mountains surround Jerusalem, so the LORD surrounds his people.*" So, I need to say to all lovers of the Bible, you can trust the text! It is not *Fake News*.

With that, let me say that I much appreciate the opportunity to participate on this esteemed panel. I fully realize that, as the only non-family member on the panel today, I will offer some contrary opinions, not only on the events of 3000 years ago, but also on today's political situation in your United States of America. Appropriately I am seated by Juan, who daily offers a contrary view on *The Five*, surrounded as he is by conservative thought. Juan, I am honored to sit by you and to offer, as you do, the lone voice of reason. I've admired your ability to be that voice, and I'll try to live up to it. You are a Democrat and I am a prophet. Democrats in your audience should be thrilled to know that theirs is the truly prophetic voice. But then, they likely know that already.

Now, the king has inquired of my views of President Trump's moving his embassy to Jerusalem. In this I must say that I agree wholeheartedly, thrilled that the city the LORD set his heart upon is recognized by your president as the capital of Israel. It is that, so I am extremely thankful that Mr. Trump has at long last recognized it to be so. Previous presidents likewise recognized it to be so, but did not deem it wise to make the move official. In this your president chose what is right over what seemed expedient. Kudos!

I must say, though, I'm rather surprised that my once, and bliss-fully former, king agrees! Were he ruler today I think he would surely move the capital to the coast, to Tel Aviv with its towering, gleaming skyscrapers. As he has this evening freely admitted, even boasted, he was always about being practical. This was the king's grave mistake, to allow economic concerns to overrule theological realities.

Jeroboam and I lived in a time when no business enterprise could have imagined their buildings growing taller than the city's places of worship. In *Yerushalayim* that highest place was the pinnacle of the temple, known in your New Testament story, I think Matthew 4, of Jesus' hunger-induced dream while fasting in the Judean desert. That dream amounted to a suicide dare from *diabolos* to cast himself down from the *"pinnacle of the temple"* in order to prove God's protection of his anointed. That rock at the pinnacle of the temple has recently been discovered in the ruins of Jerusalem, midst the pile rocks cast down from the temple in the Roman invasion of 70 A. D. That very rock at the pinnacle, inscribed with the Hebrew, "*The Trumpeting Place,*" was discovered in 1968 by archaeologist Benjamin Mazar and is today on display in Jerusalem's Israel Museum.

You see, faith was the center of life in our day, occupying the very highest point, the peak, of our living in community. Not so today, of course. Buildings centered on faith, such as temples and churches and mosques, stand deep in the shadows of the economic state. That, my friends, is the very world Jeroboam was advocating already three millennia ago. So, yes, Tel Aviv seems to me his logical choice, the city where the buildings that scrape the skies are commercial, towering over the edifices of religion. Your majesty, I would have thought Tel Aviv would be your city, so good for you. At least in the American Embassy question, you got something right.

This, though, is one of the very few things upon which we will agree. Sort of like that Never-Trumper *New York Times* columnist, Bret Stephens who, while consistently castigating Trump with a prophetic clarity I find refreshing and delightful, wrote a wonderful piece the very week of the embassy's move praising the rightness of Trump's decision. I like that Bret Stephens! He reminds of me, well, honestly, he reminds me of me. A truthteller. A prophet. He knows this man Trump, that despite his occasional ability to get something right, he is utterly wrong for your country and for world.

There are, I'll admit, a few other things on which Jeroboam and I agree. Solomon's abuses through his extravagances were, in fact, repulsive. In this I, in fact, was the first to instruct Jeroboam. He has spoken of draining the swamp, but he has me to thank that he didn't become part of the swamp himself! Without my counsel, he might have continued in Solomon's administration as one of the government's top officials.

In addition, and quite obviously, who could disagree with what Jeroboam has said of the ineffective weakness of Solomon's son? Still, I'm quite sure I would have found a more dignified way to express his character flaws than by introducing the toxicity of childish name-calling such as *Low I. Q. Rehoboam*. Unnecessary, demeaning language, if you ask me, and much too Trump-like. In this, Jeroboam is showing himself a doppelganger of your president.

Where, then did we part ways? I'll tell you in a single word, *Yerushalayim*! At our very first encounter when I, in a prayer-induced trance, sought out Jeroboam on the road, I was crystal clear that the LORD intended for Jeroboam's new kingdom never to forsake Jerusalem. I told him that the people of the ten tribes must be allowed to continue to make pilgrimage to the Holy City. I offered no alternatives, nor did I express myself with a smidgen of ambiguity. This he knew well.

He has characterized his building of shrines in Dan and Bethel as an act of pragmatism and common sense. So it may have been, but is common sense always the best path? It wasn't common sense for me to rip up my new cloak, either, but it was what the LORD commanded me to do. That was an expensive new coat, by the way, one of a precious few extravagances my life of meager means as a public servant allowed me to have. Had I not been in a trance, filled with *Ruach Elohim*, the Spirit of God, surely I would have come up with a ten count of something different. Acorns beside the road, I suppose, would have sufficed, since the whole idea of challenging a ruler as powerful as Solomon seemed to be nuts.

I jest, of course, but not in this, that we serve a God whose ways are above our ways, as far as the heaven is from the earth. That's why common sense, man's wisdom – that which prompted Jeroboam to build the accursed thing he has today called his Wall -- is not sufficient. God often chooses what seems foolishness, as your Apostle of Jesus named Paul stressed so passionately in his letter to the Corinthians, how *"it pleased God through the foolishness of preaching to save."* I love it that the word for *foolishness* in the Greek New Testament, *moria*, is the ancestor of your English word, *moron*. God is unafraid, it seems, of the moronic. Evidently America was likewise unafraid of the moronic, electing Donald Trump.

I suppose Jeroboam thought me the moron, preaching to him how critical was this matter of Jerusalem. He must have thought it foolishness to allow his tribes to continue their pilgrimages to Jerusalem, so he chose common sense over divine revelation, which is to say that he chose fear over faith. Yes, fear, the very word, I think, which is the title of one of the most critical books about your own president, by Bob Woodward, another prophet in high standing, if you ask me. I wish I had written such a book about Jeroboam, because it was precisely that, fear, that caused him to build those cursed altars you are calling Jeroboam's Wall. Can there be any doubt that, like Jeroboam's Wall, Trump's Wall is prompted by irrational fear?

If it seemed to Jeroboam obvious that allowing the people to continue allegiance to Jerusalem would eventually turn the people's hearts back to Rehoboam, it only seemed obvious through the lens of fear. The lens of faith would have sharpened focus on a different reality. I mean to say that what could have happened would have been two nations sharing one city as the center of their faith. This would not have been impossible, however true it may be that the Muslims and the Jews have not yet found a way to do the same in today's Jerusalem, despite decades of the so-called "peace process."

This fact of a divided Jerusalem even today may seem, yes, to validate the fear that King Jeroboam displayed. Understandable it is, but forgivable it is not, since he heard the word of the LORD and chose to disobey. Great faith in God and great love for God would have overcome fear. Jeroboam could not muster such faith, nor such love.

I called for faith on the road that day, not pragmatism, faith that God would overrule natural inclinations in the hearts of the people, so that they could maintain their religious core in Jerusalem while being loyal to their new political core in Shechem, Jeroboam's first capital. His failure was a failure of faith. Around this table you have heralded his business credentials, and I will not deny his remarkable gifts in that arena. I only say that it is precisely that which made him forget that God is in control of the human heart. What controlled Jeroboam's heart was power and greed.

I do not argue Jeroboam's assertion that his "Wall" was successful in accomplishing his purposes. I won't deny it. He rightly points out that all of Israel's kings following him maintained his wall policy. I simply believe that God's power would have accomplished the same purpose without the wall. Make no mistake, as soon as he erected those golden calves in Dan and Bethel, walling in his new nation and culture, he was (as you have said) *Doomed from the Start*. How could it have been otherwise? Those golden calves led the people to worship the idols of the Canaanites and to break the commandment of God.

I ask you this. Was Rehoboam stupid by not listening to his older advisors? Jeroboam has declared him so, a point the Hebrew text itself makes clear. But can't the same be said of Jeroboam? If only he had listened to me! I was his older, wiser counselor. He didn't seek me out for advice until years later when his son was on his deathbed. His neglect of my words was as consequential as Rehoboam's neglecting his advisors' counsel. So forgive me if when Jeroboam talks about *Low I. Q. Rehoboam,* I can only hear hypocrisy.

Pragmatic, yes. But, smart? Hardly. For an example of his lack of brains, I always wondered, "*Why golden calves*?" At first glance it seems he wanted to be regarded as the new nation's Moses figure. But if he knew the story of Moses and Aaron in the Exodus, and no doubt he did, why erect golden calves? This was no honorable moment in Moses' life. Far from it! If his intent was to proclaim himself a new Moses, a hero of the people delivering them from oppression, how dumb was his choice of golden calves! Did he forget that it was his brother Aaron, not Moses, who had made the idols? Did he forget that Moses condemned and destroyed the calves? Did he forget that the people were punished by God for brazen idolatry? I never understood.

Or, perhaps I did. I think his act was purely a business decision, he ever the businessman. I think it was an effort to assimilate the local Canaanite fertility cults into his own, thus increasing his base, much in the same way Democrats are accused today of wanting open borders in order to amass greater numbers in their voting bloc. The golden calves would have helped him achieve that as the Canaanites would have seen in this new king an openness to their ancient religions, he guilty of the same sin I have tonight charged to his predecessor, Solomon.

Freed from the traditions of faith centered in Jerusalem, building a "wall" to separate his people from those rich traditions of our Hebrew faith, Jeroboam found himself free to create a new faith, an amalgam of Hebrew and Canaanite traditions. What better way to strengthen the economy than to enlarge his tax base?

I've come at last to the point I've really wanted to make. Jeroboam has talked about *Dawn* and *Dusk*, ad nauseum. This theme didn't just occur to him in preparation for this visit to *The Five*. It was his drumbeat 3000 years ago, his campaign slogan, if you will. But c'mon, was he really born at dusk on the day of the temple's dedication by Solomon? Or, was this simply concocted as a battle cry? We didn't have courthouses and birth certificates back then, but if we did, I could have make quite the "Birther" claim! What if, after all, Jeroboam is the actual purveyor of *Fake News*?

He's suggested this evening that had we been speaking English 3,000 years ago he would have had a symbol for his campaign, the two Ds of *Dawn* and *Dusk* facing each other and interlocking to create a threshold, a door of hope which he opened and through which he led the ten tribes. I agree that the symbol is memorable, even powerful. But, know this. I was the only one present at both Jeroboam's *Dawn* and his *Dusk*, politically speaking. I was the King-maker, and I was the King-breaker.

I mentioned the Canaanite assimilation which I suspect Jeroboam's Wall was really all about. Did you know that within Canaanite mythology was a well-known story of two half-brother gods known as *Dawn* and Dusk? It's true. I suspect it was that very pagan myth which was the inspiration for his *Fake News*.

Your archaeologists discovered a cache of Canaanite myths in the 1920s in Ugarit, also known as Ras Shamra, in northern Syria on the coast of the Mediterranean. One of those myths was called the *Birth of the Gracious Gods*. In this vile story, the old senile God heading the pantheon, El, is relaxing on the beach. In a test of his virility he is seduced by two goddesses. In a fertility-based religion such as the Canaanites, the god cannot be suspected as suffering from erectile dysfunction. In our time, there were no blue pills or chews to remedy that condition.

The language of this myth is rather X-rated and perhaps too graphic for your audience but, bottom line, El proves himself and succeeds in impregnating both women. These women both conceive and give birth, simultaneously, to half-brothers, *Shahir (Dawn)* and *Shalim (Dusk)*. So, instead of Jeroboam's interlocking Ds, I suggest a different image, interlocking the two Canaanite Ss of *Shahir* and *Shalim* so that you can see the snake he really was, the spiraling, coiling, striking snake of sin. Those two Ss form the swastika, a symbol very much in the dialogue of today's political debate in your country, comparing your president to Hitler.

Dawn and Dusk, indeed. Just as the dawn of Adolf Hitler was the dusk of freedom in Europe, so the dawn of Jeroboam was the dusk of godliness in the Galilee and throughout the territory of the ten tribes. Likewise, I think, the dawn of Donald J. Trump has become the dusk of what once was good about America.

By the way, if Jeroboam rejoices in his victory over the House of David, I find it deliciously ironic that the only archaeological evidence ever found referring to the House of David was discovered right there in Dan, by the king's northern "Wall." The David Inscription, produced about 100 years after Jeroboam's death while the kingdom was still strong, was discovered at Tel Dan in the 1993-1994 season by archaeologist Avriham Biran. You have to love it that the House of David's reach through time extended all the way to Jeroboam's Wall!

Dan is a beautiful place in the northern Galilee, today wedged precariously between the borders of Syria to the east and Lebanon to the west, modern day enemies of Israel. One of the headwaters of the Jordan River flows by Dan with refreshing waters from Mount Hermon. Tourists today visit the Dan Nature Center before they enter the ruins, and soon find themselves standing at Jeroboam's *bamah*, or high place, the very platform upon which Jeroboam built and placed his accursed golden calf. Our history comes alive in few places more than at that spot, though today it is wonderful that our history is coming alive on *The Five*. Thank you for allowing us this opportunity to tell one of the Bible's most important stories, a story oddly neglected and therefore untold by popular avenues of commentary, art, and entertainment.

Now, my time is short, and I know that those in your audience familiar with the biblical story will be wishing for me to comment on the second part of the Jeroboam story in which I play a key role. You've heard how I was present at the beginning of Jeroboam's story, told in 1 Kings 11. Many years later, a story told in chapter 14, I again played a key role in the king's life, a scene worthy of your most intense and climactic movie moments.

When Jeroboam's son, Abijah, fell ill, who did he come running to for help? Me, of course. By this time I was an old man and blind. Jeroboam sent his wife, Ano, in disguise with, get this, ten loaves! Ten loaves along with a jar of preserves. Imagine! As if a gift of ten to the once giver of ten would change the fate of his suffering son. And, for God's sake, why don a disguise? How would a disguise help in trying to trick a blind man?

I was blind, though, only in the flesh, for the LORD was with me, saying "*Jeroboam's wife is coming to consult about her son, for he is sick.*" What God told me to tell her was going to break her heart and, in truth, broke my heart as well.

My favorite painting of this moment, by the way, was by the 17th century French artist, Frans van Mieris, now at the Palais de Beaux-Arts de Lille. It shows how shocked she was when, at the very sound of her footsteps at the threshold, I shouted, "*Come in, Ano! Why are in disguise?*" I realize that in the Hebrew text the historians replaced my calling to her by her name, Ano, with the generic, "*Come in, wife of Jeroboam.*" While I have defended the historians' overall assessment of Jeroboam, I admit that historians are not without their slant. Ano's name is only mentioned in the Septuagint. The Hebrew historians from Judah wanted the text to regard her as only a beautiful foreign appendage to a sinful king. They wanted history to see Ano as detached, perhaps even ashamed of her husband, and so presented her as a flat and vapid person. That was their aim in removing her name from the text. Lost to the generations is how very charming and intelligent she was. In truth, I was heartbroken having to convey the message of the Lord to Ano regarding her son's fate.

Van Mieris's painting shows a little white lap dog between Ano and me, as if protecting me from poor Ano. It reminds me of a little Maltese with a puppy cut, yapping with feeble ferocity. That's my favorite element in the painting because if my message was full of fury, it was a fury for Jeroboam, not for Ano, whom I rather admired. I wished her no more harm than that little puppy could have done to her.

I was condemning Jeroboam's treachery, his bringing of molten images into the consciousness of the people. I declared that God would punish the House of Jeroboam by cutting them off from the land of the living. Though my words to her were harsh and scathing in tone, my heart for her was soft. Even prophets, perhaps especially prophets, hurt for the people who are hurting under their condemnation. No, that dog had no bite. At least, not for her.

I sent her away, saying, "*Go home! As you step inside the city, your child will die, for he alone of Jeroboam's house is loved by God. So he will die and be buried, and not suffer what the rest of the dynasty of Jeroboam is destined to suffer.*"

It's surely one of the saddest pictures in the Bible. Does she cross the threshold of the city to hear the wails of the people's mourning in the death of their prince, or does she prolong his suffering by staying outside the city, hoping against hope for the LORD to change his decree?

CHAPTER SIX

Ano, the wife of Jeroboam

————————

Jedediah: Well, at last we've come all the way around the table to Ano, the gorgeous Egyptian wife of Jeroboam. Queen Ano, Ahijah has left us hanging in an intense scenario, you traveling home after hearing the prophecy that your son will die upon your arrival. Will you tell us more about your son, about what you felt as your journeyed back home?

Ano: Good evening, Jedediah. As you know, I was not a Hebrew speaker from birth, being Egyptian, yet I know that yours is a beautiful Hebrew name meaning, *"Beloved of the LORD."* And so you must surely be! Thank-you for every kindness you have shown me tonight as your guest.

Perhaps you're aware that God himself gave your very name, Jedediah, to a very special newborn infant whom he loved. Do you know what child that was? It was Solomon. It's true, King David's son,

Solomon, was actually named Jedediah. The prophet Nathan "*chris-tened*" him, as you might say today of a child's naming ceremony, as a child beloved by the LORD, this second son of David and Bathsheba. Their first child, born of David's adultery, died as an infant according to the word of the same prophet Nathan who, pointing the accusing finger at David declared, "*Thou art the man!*"

It's the same message, you might say, that I received from Ahijah the prophet, the message I was to carry to my husband. "*Thou art the man!*" As David and Bathsheba lost their firstborn, so also did Jeroboam and Ano. Our precious son, Abijah, according to the word of the prophet, died. The prophet had pointed at my husband the accusing finger, delivering to me his dreadful message that my son would die upon my return home to Tirzah. Though a short journey home from Shiloh, barely 10 miles, it was a most difficult journey, as you might imagine.

I was not a follower of the Hebrew God, having grown up with my own gods in Egypt, but I always deeply respected, even feared, my husband's God. My journey home was filled, at first, with angry prayer, but as we drew closer to Tirzah my mood strangely calmed. More than calmed, I think. I became numb, my spirit carrying me into an oddly thin place, by which I mean a place where the veil between our world and the Beyond seemed porous, as if one were leaking into the other. It was as if I had only to put my foot across the threshold from this to that Other world where geography is needless, all places immediately present. In such a grief-induced trance, Tirzah seemed to grow more distant even as we drew nearer its gates, and yet oddly present at the same time, making pointless my steps. I would arrive, I knew, soon enough. Sooner than I wished.

My husband had three capitals, by the way. You may think of Shechem, where it all started, as something like Trump Tower in New York. We used it as our palace while building and fortifying the actual capital, Tirzah, the equivalent of your White House in Washington.

Tirzah is mentioned in *Shir ha-sharrim*, the Song of Songs, romantic poetry your audience will know better as the Song of Solomon. Just after what are perhaps the song's most beautiful words, *ani le-dodi ve-dodi li* (*I am my beloved's and my beloved is mine*), one reads, "*You are beautiful as Tirzah, my love, comely as Jerusalem.*" The Song of Songs, you see, links the capitals of Judah (Jerusalem) and of Israel (Tirzah). Wonderful, isn't it, how poetry can achieve what politics is powerless to do?

My husband built our third capital city, Penuel, meaning "*Face of God*," in the TransJordan near the Jabbok River where Jacob wrestled with the angel. You may think of our third capital as you would of the president's Florida escape, Mar-a-Lago. As Mr. Trump and the First Lady must love their visits to Mar-a-lago, so we loved our visits to Penuel. Had we golf back then, I could have designed a beautiful course along the Jabbok. I've come to think that a golf course is one of the few ways humans can design something improving upon creation's natural beauty, especially at dawn and dusk, the landscape glistening with the morning dew or tinted by the hues of the setting sun. Beautifully manicured links seem to me a true Penuel, an image of the face of God.

I apologize for digressing. We were, as you know, in the palace at Tirzah when Abijah fell ill. The trip to Shiloh was not a long trip, as I have said, only some 12 miles. Before I describe my arrival in Tirzah, let me first say how much I appreciate Ahijah's kind words a moment ago. I felt, and deeply, the concern he held for me and my son, his compassion leaking through his forceful condemnation. He was saying of my husband, "*Thou art the man!*" not of me, "*Thou art the woman!*" I understood that, even as I fully believed the prophet's word that my son would die as I crossed the threshold into Tirzah. I expected never to hold my son again.

Messengers ran ahead of my entourage to inform my husband of the situation. I suppose I hoped he would bring our son to the gates of Tirzah so that I could at least see him, whisper my love to him across the threshold before he died. Perhaps, I wondered, it would only be my feet that would trigger his death, allowing me to trick providence, to slip my hand and my heart across, into the city undetected and unchallenged. I would gladly have set up a tent to live three feet from the gate, my feet never crossing, if I might only hold him every day in my outstretched arms. But that act of my selfishness would only have prolonged his suffering, which was great.

We arrived in mid-afternoon on a cold and wet winter day. I expected that when I entered the city, wails of mourning would fill the air. The prophet's words have a high drama about them, don't they? I am a lover of your cinema and confess that I wonder how it is that no film has yet portrayed that moment or, at least, none of which I'm aware.

In reality, though, what happened wasn't so dramatic. I suppose that the prophet's words as recorded in the Hebrew text may be understood to have been written like your movies portraying a story *"based on actual events."* What I mean is, while there is truth, there is also dramatic license. In fact, while the prophet had said my son would die as soon as I entered the city, only a few verses later the text says my son died at the moment I crossed the threshold into the *beit,* or the house.

So which is it, the city or the house? Already the text admits to a slight discrepancy, but the actual discrepancy was much greater. In fact, I arrived in time to hold my son for three full days prior to his death. I considered those three days to be the mercy of God extended to me in answer to my fervent prayer. I don't mean to suggest that the Bible's account is *Fake News* even though, read literally, it is. No, but rather I see it as artistic flair, an embellishment of what actually happened. It was true, though, in this respect, my son's death was a terrible threshold moment for me, for my husband the king, and for our nation.

As has been more than once mentioned I, like your First Lady, was multi-lingual. To explain what I feel about Ahijah's prophecy I will use one of my favorite French terms, *l'esprit de l'escalier.* It means *"the wit of the staircase"* or, perhaps easier for your English speakers to see, *"the spirit of the escalator."*

Have you ever been in a conversation when you were at a loss for words, only to think of what you should have said, what you might have said, as you were walking down the stairs to leave? Of course you have. We all have! Each of us, even tonight, after the cameras go dark, will recall how we might have phrased our point more precisely, more impactfully.

Here's the catch, though. In the weeks and years ahead, as you remember the conversation, you begin to remember, not what you actually said, but what you thought later to say, after the opportunity had passed. That is *l'esprit de l'escalier*, memory riding an escalator so that at last you remember as truth not what actually happened, but what might have happened if you had had your wits about you. *L'esprit de l'escalier.* Isn't it a beautiful concept, and doesn't it resonate with undeniable truth that our memories are fragile reconstructions?

I thought of this watching the confirmation hearings of Judge Brett Kavanaugh to the Supreme Court, challenged by accusations of vile sexual misconduct when a teenager nearly forty years previous. I wondered, listening, as all must have, who is telling the truth? Who is lying? But what if both were telling the truth as they recall it, both truths having taken a ride on the escalator of their memories?

That's what the text does with this dramatic moment in my life, a mother losing her child. Oh, there was drama enough in my son's death without the threshold element being overplayed. My heart felt it keenly, I assure you. So, I think it matters not that my son's death didn't occur the very moment my foot crossed the threshold of the city, or of the house. The fact is, his death was a threshold moment for me, a stepping into the uncharted territory of agonizing grief, something no parent should ever have to do, peasant or princess. I was Princess Ano, the daughter of Pharaoh Shishak, and now I was Queen Ano, wife of King Jeroboam. My life had been one of privilege, a succession of astonishments. And now, this. My son was dead, my status useless to immunize me from grief.

I said that I appreciate the prophet's kind words about his feelings for me while delivering his devastating message. As I look back on our brief visit, there are many things I wish I had said to him, ranging from an outburst of royal rage to a plea for mercy. I, though, who speak so many languages, could find no words. There was nothing to say, so I said nothing. I left with a certain numbness of soul devoid of either anger or further appeals. My son would die. I knew it now, irreversibly.

Yet, he had told me that my son was dying because God loved him, sparing him the agony to be endured by the rest of the House of Jeroboam. What strange comfort those words were to me.

But how could God do this to my son, my innocent son? At that moment I hated that we had named him Abijah, meaning *My Father is Yahweh*, for what father would kill his son while professing love? Only an insane one. Even Abraham stayed his hand so that Isaac lived. In that moment, I would have preferred an Egyptian name for my son. My Egyptian deities were kinder, or at least I had thought so.

In the days of grief that followed, one of my maids recalled for me a Hebrew story of an earlier prophet of Shiloh and how he, too, was visited by a famous wife from the tribe of Ephraim, a woman who was seeking God's blessing for a son. That prophet's name was Eli, the grandfather of our own Ahijah, and the woman who visited Eli was Hannah, the wife of Elkanah.

If the twilight twins of *Dawn* and *Dusk* has been a recurring theme today, let me say that I think our two biblical stories, Hannah's and Ano's, are just such twins. Two Ephramite wives visiting two prophets of Shiloh. More than twins, those two stories are *Dawn* and *Dusk* stories, by which I mean to say that she, Hannah, was the *Dawn* and that I, Ano, was the *Dusk*.

In their annual pilgrimage to Shiloh to make sacrifice, Hannah, who was barren, went to the temple to pray for a son, vowing that if given a son she would offer him to the LORD as a Nazarite, one making a vow of abstinence from both wine and the razor. When she arrived at Shiloh she was distressed, praying fervently. Eli observed her lips moving without making a sound and thought her intoxicated. Angry, he said, *"How long will you make a drunken spectacle of yourself?"*

When Hannah declared that she was not drunk but vexed in spirit because of her barrenness, Eli blessed her, embarrassed at his own mistake. Hannah, now blessed, conceived and bore a son, naming him Samuel, meaning *"God has heard."* This beautiful story is told in 1 Samuel 1. Samuel became the *Dawn* of a new era in Hebrew history, a transitional figure who, unlike my husband, consolidated rather than divided the twelve tribes of Israel. It was this very Samuel who anointed Israel's first two kings, Saul and David.

After my handmaiden shared this story with me, I inquired more of that period of history, which had occurred over a century earlier. You have heard tonight of the eerie similarities of Jeroboam ben Nebat and Donald J. Trump. Let me now share with you the uncanny dissimilarities of two Ephraimite wives visiting two prophets of Shiloh.

Hannah went to Shiloh to pray, having no intention of meeting the prophet, much less of deceiving him. I, on the other hand, traveled to Shiloh intent on an audience with the prophet, and on deception.

Hannah's intent was to pray for the birth of a son. My intent was to avoid the death of my son.

Hannah was a commoner. I was royalty.

Hannah's actions were carried out in transparency before a prophet who was young and could see clearly. Yet, still, he misjudged Hannah. My actions were disguised, yet even an old and blind prophet saw right through me.

And, at last, Hannah gained a son, rejoicing in her *Dawn*, while I lost my son, so that the darkness of *Dusk* enveloped me.

My study discovered even more, how Elkanah, distressed over his beloved wife's despair over her barrenness, had declared his love for her by saying, *"Am I not more to you that ten sons?"* There it is again, that number we have heard throughout this night, *The Ten*! What is it about that number? The prophet tearing his garment to give my husband ten pieces. God giving my husband ten tribes. I taking ten loaves. Now I read of Elkanah promising Hannah that he would be for her more than ten sons. Reading of all these tens, it's like it was all planned, scripted, nothing left to chance, all my Dawns and all my Dusks under the sovereign control of a God whom I did not know.

I thought of how Samuel, Hannah's son, grew to anoint Saul as king, but then sought out David in Bethlehem when Saul lost God's favor. And I wondered, could this Hebrew God be so fickle and changing, his plan so easily altered? How is it that so many divine dawns of a new day so swiftly darken?

My mother-in-law's dream of her son bringing dusk upon Israel was very real to me. A darkness was entering my soul, I who was born into royalty as a Princess of Egypt, raised with boundless privilege. As a child I imagined that being a royal was all light and no darkness, while the lot of common people was darkness with but little light. How wrong I was! The vicissitudes of life are harsh instructors for each one of the human family, as true of the royal Ano as of the commoner, Hannah, and as true of Queen Ano as of First Lady Melania; as true of Solomon as of Obama; of Rehoboam as of Hillary; as true of Jeroboam as of Trump; each pairing whose similarities have been placed side-by-side tonight.

To those political pairings I will add the most essential similarity of all. Each have their *Dawn*, their birth, and each have their *Dusk*, their death. *C'est la vie!*

> *Nature's first green is gold,*
> *Her hardest hue to hold,*
> *Her early leaf's a flower,*
> *But only so an hour.*
> *Then leaf subsides to leaf,*
> *so Eden sank to grief,*
> *so dawn goes down to day,*
> *Nothing gold can stay.*

Oh, how I love your Frost! *"Dawn goes down to day,"* indeed! Nothing gold can stay, whether the golden splendor of royalty, or of temples, or of life itself. All of it is only for an hour. Nothing gold can stay, not even my husband's golden calves.

The awareness of this makes me smile at the polarizing passion of the political sides, in my day and in yours. Neither amounts to much in comparison with what really matters, which is what I felt so intensely in those three days holding my dying son, my own painful Pieta. During those three days of my son's dying and death my soul knew as never before that what really matters is love, the kind of love that brightens our days when our walk is well and darkens our heart when wellness fades into a distant mirage.

Now, if I may before I finish, it occurs to me that I began my story as cued by the prophet, at the end of my son's life. May I say something about a much earlier time, a much brighter time in the lives of King Jeroboam and Queen Ano?

Jedediah: Please do, Queen Ano. Take us back to Egypt.

Ano: What an unlikely story is ours, the daughter of Pharaoh wed to the son of a widow from a small and poor village in Ephraim. He has mentioned that he fled to Egypt for asylum when he was but 28. I was younger still, only 18. Of course, you must know that I was deeply drawn to him from the moment I saw him. How strikingly handsome this Jeroboam ben Nebat was to look upon!

My father called him *"Schlomo's Rebel,"* the Hebrew pronunciation of the name you know as Solomon. My father, of course, was always looking for advantageous political alliances. That's what kings do, right?

It's at the top of their job description. Why, exactly, this might be called collusion, as in your present political intrigue, escapes me. It seems to me that those with skill to broker such alliances deserve to rule and have the best chance to rule successfully. Hardly a disqualifying quality.

While *Schlomo's Rebel* came to us with no political power, a young exile from the reigning monarch of the House of David, pharaoh saw something extraordinary in him. Goodness, we all did. How could anyone miss it? His physique, his charisma, his elegance. He was the entire package, and it took no time at all for pharaoh to see why Solomon had raised him so quickly to a position of power in his government.

My husband mentioned an earlier rebel against David and Solomon whom my father took in, Hadad the Edomite. Uncle Hadad came to us many years before I was born. Like my husband, he was taken in by my father and made a royal by marrying my aunt, the queen's older sister.

I heard that when the news came that King David had died, Uncle Hadad appealed to my father about going back to Israel to challenge Solomon, he in the tender first moments of his reign. My father did not think the timing propitious, so dissuaded him. After that, if my uncle continued to harbor a wish to go back to Israel, it gradually faded.

The Bible is correct in saying that his son, my first cousin Genubath, grew up in the palace with the children of pharaoh. Genubath was ten years older than I, the same age as Jeroboam. Had God's providence turned only slightly, I suppose it could have been Uncle Hadad returning to Israel to claim the throne and my cousin Genubath with him as prince and future monarch of Israel. Oddly enough, Genubath had a thing for me, so I might still have been queen of Israel, in either scenario! Still, isn't it amazing how throughout history the fortunes of Egypt and Israel have so often been intertwined.

My father had greater plans for Jeroboam than he could ever realize with my Uncle Hadad. If the timing for my uncle had not been good, it was perfect for my husband. Knowing that Solomon was growing old, my father now saw an opportunity to disrupt Israel's political stability, perhaps even to place a family member on the throne of Israel.

Through me Jeroboam had become an Egyptian royal. I loved him, though I wasn't at first sure I could love him. Despite having been an official in Solomon's kingdom he was, after all, not a royal. He was a mason. "*Curator of the walls of Jerusalem*," as Josephus said of him, a builder. How could I love such a common man?

One of my favorite literary works growing up in the royal court was from nearly a thousand years before I was born. Scholars know it today as *The Satire of the Trades*, and I must admit that I thought of it when father first told me I would be given as wife to this famous builder of walls.

The Satire of the Trades is a didactic work from the Middle Kingdom in which a scribe named Dua-Khety is advising his son, Pepi, on what to be when he grows up. Pepi's father wants his son to follow him in being a scribe, so that his son might one day be able to enjoy the benefits of mastering the highest technology of the day. The work resonates even today, doesn't it, for what father wouldn't want this for his son?

The humor comes as this father is deliberately derisive of all trades except the scribal profession. He begins, *"I'll make you love scribe-dom more than your mother, I'll make its beauties stand out for you! It's the greatest of all callings. There's none like it in the land."* He ends by saying, *"See, there's no profession without a boss, except for the scribe; he is the boss. Hence, if you know writing, it will do better for you than all those professions I've set before you, each more wretched than the other."*

Between this beginning and ending he lists the occupations, hilariously exaggerating their misery. For example, he says, *"I never saw a sculptor as an envoy, but I have seen him at work, his fingers like the claws of a crocodile, and he stinks more than fish roe."* He speaks also of the barber moving from street to street looking for someone's hair to cut, *"straining his arms to fill his belly."*

He makes fun of the reed-cutter in the delta areas, *"slain by mosquitos and slaughtered by gnats."* Of the gardener he says that his shoulders are bent with age, working himself to death more than all the other professions, and of the fisherman that it's the *"worst of all jobs,"* working in the midst of crocodiles.

Then he turns to the mason, which is of course why I thought of Jeroboam. *"His loins give him pain and though he works outside in the wind he works without a cloak. His loincloth is a twisted rope and a string covers his buttocks."*

I smile, a bit embarrassed to admit that when first introduced to this Jeroboam the Wall-builder I had a picture of him in my mind wearing a G-string, exposing his rear. Honestly, though, he was so magnificent that the thought gave me pleasure, and with that I shall stop before I further dishonor myself.

Our courtship was brief, but proper, despite the impure thoughts I've just now confessed. Our love became the inspiration of Pharaoh's court poets and musicians:

> *Schlomo's rebel has fled the king's murderous hand,*
>
> *Running, this ben Nebat to Egypt-land.*
>
> *Jeroboam of Princess Ano learns.*
>
> *Ben Nebat for Princess Ano yearns.*
>
> *Schlomo's rebel pledges a love as enduring as the sun,*
>
> *in Egypt-land or in the north, where'eer they run.*

You're smiling. It's not much in English, I admit. I've translated to provide the rhyme you English speakers expect of poetry but, truth be told, all writing loses nuances of meaning in translation, rhyme or no rhyme. O, but you should have heard it sung at our royal wedding with the background instruments supplied by Pharaoh's most accomplished musicians. There was such celebration that day, even for my alcohol-abstaining husband.

I knew it might happen that we would return to Jerusalem. In truth, though, I suppose I imagined, perhaps even hoped, that we would be in my very Egypt our entire lives, like my Uncle Hadad whom I had known all my life. His life lacked for nothing in Egypt, and I would have gladly lived such a life with Jeroboam as Egyptian royalty.

Yes, my husband was a royal now, a gift to him from pharaoh, but it was in no way certain that he would return to Israel. Not only had Uncle Hadad stayed in Egypt, but that earlier Hebrew, Joseph, never went home until his descendants carried his bones back, he serving pharaoh throughout his days.

I wondered if the same might hold true for my husband. Perhaps, but I knew he passionately dreamed of return, and that should that moment arrive, he would return to Israel as royalty with pharaoh's blessing.

And so it came to pass that, after only two years, he was called home. I was 20 when we got word of Schlomo's death. My husband, now 30, went ahead of me for haste as my attendants prepared to accompany me on a later journey. After an appropriate period to say goodbye to my mother and father, and to my very Egypt, my entourage left to join my husband.

Our path would not, of course, take us along the Via Maris and up to Jerusalem through Lachish. That would be far too dangerous at this politically charged moment. No, but we were to travel the longer route, circling east only to turn north at the Gulf of Aqaba, towards the Dead Sea's west shore and up the Jordan River valley, bypassing Jerusalem entirely.

Messengers from my husband, by then the crowned king of Israel, reached our entourage just as we were readying to turn north. They advised that we should circle on an even wider route, all the way to the King's Highway beyond the Jordan so that our northward trek would be on the eastern side of the Sea, through Edom and Moab, avoiding the territory of Judah. It struck me that we would now follow the path of an earlier Hebrew who, like my husband, had been made an Egyptian royal, Moses.

We came very close to Petra, by the way, the place your American tourists flock to today to see this mysterious rose red city carved out of the sandstone. This is the place where Sean Connery and Harrison Ford played out the final scene in *Indiana Jones and the Last Crusade*.

As you can tell, I do love your cinema!

CHAPTER SEVEN

The Second Hour
Juan Points to the Elephant in the Studio

Juan: Queen Ano, I've studied the biblical story of Jeroboam in preparation for tonight and noted that the Bible's historians allow us to hear not a single word from your mouth. Not one word. You are, in the text, utterly silent. I find that, after listening to you tonight, both remarkable and sad. How different and fun you are in person, an absolute delight!

Thank you for sharing your story, and thanks to each one of our special guests this evening on *The Five*. Our regular viewers realize how very special, and unorthodox, this edition of *The Five* is. You've made a rather obscure biblical story come alive for us by drawing fascinating parallels between your king and our president, not to mention similarities between Queen Ano and First Lady Melania Trump, between

King Solomon and President Obama, between Rehoboam and Hillary, and more.

It's time now, in the second hour of our special edition, for Greg, Dana, Jesse, Jedediah, and me to get more involved by offering our own comments and asking questions of our guests in the round robin interview style familiar to our viewers.

I'll get right to it by addressing what I think is a very large elephant in this studio, which is this: Are we to think of Jeroboam as a villain or a hero? The Old Testament clearly paints him as a villain. To consider him a hero renders the biblical account Fake News. Each of our guests, other than Ahijah, have done precisely that, asserting that the Bible's account concerning Jeroboam is slanted in an unfair and biased fashion. Greg, in his opening monologue, even described the biblical narrative as exhibiting symptoms of *Jeroboam Derangement Syndrome,* a phrase meant to exonerate Jeroboam in the same way *Trump Derangement Syndrome* seeks to exonerate Trump. It seems to me that Greg, by labeling the Bible's words as deranged in his opening monologue, opened the door wide for this elephant to enter.

How so? Well, because so many of President Trump's supporters are evangelical Christians. To gain any sense of satisfaction in the comparisons made tonight between these two wall-builders, Jeroboam and Trump, these evangelical supporters of the president must be willing to think of their beloved Bible in the same way President Trump thinks of *Fake News CNN.* I don't think they're ready or willing, or even able, to do that. Seems to me that the comparisons we've made this evening equate CNN and the mainstream media with the Bible itself, both deranged!

Which is why I think the president's evangelical supporters must be severely conflicted right now, seeing in Jeroboam the Wall Builder a 3,000 year old reason to cheer Trump the Would-be Wall Builder, but only if they buy into the premise that their Bible is Fake News. The Bible clearly leads its readers to dislike King Jeroboam as a perpetrator of evil. So, if we are comparing Trump to Jeroboam, wouldn't the Bible also be asking its believers to see Trump as a villain?

Nebat, you were the first guest around this table to level the Fake News charge against the Bible, so I begin with you. How can a Trump-supporting evangelical Christian see Jeroboam ben Nebat as a hero with similarities to their hero, President Trump, without sacrificing their high view of scripture? Wouldn't they prefer to keep their views of biblical inerrancy and dump this whole comparison of Trump with your son, ben Nebat?

Nebat: Juan, I am a Hebrew, a son of Abraham proud of my tribal heritage from Ephraim. As all Hebrews, I own a deep respect for the sacred text of the Tanakh, which is an abbreviation for the Hebrew Scripture's three parts: *Torah, Nevi'im, Kethuvim* (the Law, the Prophets, and the Writings). The word Tanakh is formed from the T of Torah, the N of Nevi'im, and the K of Kethuvim. Those three divisions are important to note as I answer your question.

We are, indeed, people of *ha-Sepher* (the Book), but my reverence for the sacred text does not demand that each word be accurate in the historical sense. I don't think this will come as a shock to those who love the Bible, so I strongly disagree with your conclusions about evangelicals. They, in my estimation, will not have nearly so much of a problem as you suggest in accepting my assessment of the biased and, therefore, flawed historical portions of the text.

My characterization of those sections of the Hebrew Bible as Fake News in no way challenges the rich theologies of one's faith, Jewish or Christian. The passages pertinent to our discussion are not theologically-oriented, but rather are those offering historical analysis, in the same way as the op-ed pages of your newspaper. The books of the Kings and the Chronicles are written by southern historians expressing the opinion of the one side, Judah, that outlasted the other, Israel.

I believe my son's case is the most egregious example of bias to be found in those chronicles, the utterly slanted opinion of Judah's historians. Predictably, and understandably, their writings are filled with anti-north, anti-Jeroboam prejudice. My assessment of these passages in no way compromises the deeper and sacred redemptive teachings of Holy Scripture.

The assessment of my son which Bible readers have read for these 3,000 years is similar to what future generations would think of Trump if the only commentary on his administration which they have to read for the next three millennia came from Huffington Post, Buzzfeed, or CNN. Or, conversely, imagine what future generations would think of President Obama if the only commentary surviving concerning his presidency for the next 3,000 years came from Breitbart, Fox, and the Heritage Foundation.

Juan: Okay, I see, you want us to read 1 Kings as the op-ed pages of the Bible rather than the front page. Seems to me that this leaves it up to the reader to draw a line between those sections that are divinely inspired and which sections are offered as mere human opinion, a distinction evangelicals will be loath to make, in my opinion. So, I must say that I don't agree that your answer will be found satisfactory by them. But I'll turn the question to Queen Ano. Does the wife of Jeroboam agree with her father-in-law?

Ano: I do, Juan, but I think a better analogy than *The New York Times* editorial page is Hollywood. I think of these historical sections of the Bible in the same way moviegoers regard a film inspired by historical events. They realize when they see the tagline, *"Based on actual events,"* that this is both claimer and disclaimer, that within those words is an admission that the story as it is being told is not intended to be an exact replication of moment-by-moment reality. We must make room, even in the Bible, for literary ornamentation.

However, and directly to your point, yes, some biblical literalists may be offended, wishing to stand by the literal "was-ness" of each moment as the Bible describes it. Like the bumper-sticker slogan, *"The Bible says it. I believe it. That settles it!"* I would not have allowed such a message to adorn my royal chariot, I assure you.

I say, "Lighten up!" *L'esprit de l'escalier*, remember? The actual events of history rode up the escalator through multiple tellings around tribal campfires, until the narrative at last reached the dramatic pinnacle enshrined in text. Storytelling, putting an event in a narrative format, preserves and distorts the story, all at the same time.

A good example is the narrative of my son's death, upon which I commented earlier. In this story there is no higher historical source to appeal to than to me. I was there, and I will tell you with certainty that my son didn't actually, clinically, die the second I crossed the threshold into Tirzah. As I have told you, I was granted the mercy to hold my boy for three days.

Does this make the written account Fake News? I don't think so. If you view every word of the text with wooden literalism then, yes, the inaccuracy renders the text less than factual. But, in fact, there was deeper truth expressed here, a truth leading the reader to understand the mystery of the threshold moment in each of our lives, the mezuzah moment of change when we cross a threshold from Here to There, from what was to what is.

As I approached Tirzah I assure you I wasn't humming *Que Sera Sera*, "Whatever will be, will be." I knew what would happen and I was devastated in that knowing. The threshold I crossed was from embracing my beloved son to burying him. The Bible's telling truthfully relates this terrible crossing into a deep darkness of the soul.

Abijah did, in fact and according to the word of the prophet, die. His death changed my life. I needed no excess drama such as the text offers to heighten the fear gripping me as I returned from Shiloh. But, for the reader of the story through these thousands of years, the dramatically-written text deliciously amplifies the tension, allowing them better to walk that journey with me, in the same way your films allow the viewer to enter the story and walk with the hero or the heroine.

The story as it is told in 1 Kings is Fake News only for the one whose faith requires them to regard the text as a perfect recording of moment-by-moment reality. There is no mystery in that assertion, nor is it startling to any fair mind, and I think today's evangelicals can appreciate that fact as something less than the elephant you imagine lurking about in the studio.

Juan: Okay, I turn to you, Ahijah. It was your prophecy, after all, that the wife of Jeroboam is talking about. How do you think your words should be understood by the modern reader of the Bible? Op-ed? Hollywood? Or, inerrant and infallible?

Ahijah: Did you know, Juan, that the word Abracadabra, that magical word spoken to open what is shut, derives from Hebrew? It does. Abracadabra comes from a Hebrew phrase which may be translated, *"I create what I speak."*

Now, I did prophesy that Abijah would die when Ano entered the house. Or, was it when she entered the city? Goodness, I spoke the words myself and even I can't recall! The text says both. I may have said both. My point is, it doesn't matter.

You see, even if the scribes reported my words accurately, I wasn't speaking in an *"Abracadabra"* sort of way. I wasn't suggesting that, presto, death would be instantaneous, coinciding precisely with Ano's physical movement across the threshold. Historians wrote it like that, giving it a theatrical flair, but that's not how I intended it. Their writing the story in that way makes for intense drama, an artistic exaggeration. In this Ano is correct, nor will I argue otherwise.

Still, as to your larger question, the idea put forth by Nebat that prophets and scribes were offering Fake News in their unswerving condemnations of Jeroboam's building the shrines at Dan and Bethel and of his appointing of non-Levites as priests to serve those shrines, I say emphatically that this was not Fake News, but divine truth. In this crucial element of the narrative, we've left the op-ed page and returned to the front page. The prophets were acting as true and faithful representatives of God. This outlaw of a king, whom I at first supported and lifted him into prominence, strayed from his calling and deserved but well this constant stream of condemnation about which tonight he has complained so bitterly.

I wish I had known Yeats back then. His words powerfully paint a picture of Jeroboam as I knew him, a promising young man to whom I was an instrument of God in gifting him with the greater part of Solomon's kingdom. Riding upon my words, this young falcon of a king took wing, but was soon enough . . .

> *Turning and turning in the widening gyre,*
> *The falcon cannot hear the falconer;*
> *Things fall apart; the center cannot hold;*
> *A mere anarchy is loosed upon the world.*

I was the falconer who, with inspired prophecy, launched Jeroboam on his flight. As he rose, though, he extended beyond the range of my voice, widening his circling far afield of the divine commission I had given him. It's no wonder things fell apart. It's no wonder that the center, Jerusalem, could not hold. And, when Jerusalem didn't hold as the center of the nation due to Jeroboam's sin, anarchy was loosed throughout our land.

Jeroboam: Anarchy! I think we've established already here tonight, and without argument, that my twenty-two years on the throne brought unprecedented prosperity to a people burdened with governmental malfeasance, and . . .

Ahijah: Patience, my king, blessedly no longer my king, you will have your turn to speak. I'm sure Jesse will see to that!

Juan, with the ascension of Jeroboam to the throne something insidious had been born, and while I had a role in that birth, I had not yet named its offspring. Yeats gives it a proper name at the end of his poem:

> *And what Rough Beast,*
>
> *its hour come round at last,*
>
> *slouches towards Bethlehem to be born?*

Jeroboam arose from Ephraim as a savior figure for his people, but his unconscionable actions offended God and rendered him a Rough Beast, a malignancy within Israel. I daresay that Donald, "*J for Jeroboam*" Trump, is the Rough Beast loosed upon the world today.

Fascinating, isn't it, that Yeats' poem is titled, "*The Second Coming*"? Fitting, since all we have said today exposes your president as something of a return of the calamitous and catastrophic life of the wall-builder, Jeroboam ben Nebat, who couldn't see that the walls he built separated God's people from each other. President Trump, I think, is doing the same, building walls of division throughout your country.

Jesse: Okay, and ouch! Ahijah has given me the opening to bring the king into the conversation. Juan, let's go to the king to see what he has to say about being called a Rough Beast.

Juan: Let's do, but I want to stay with my original question. Your Majesty, there is no doubt that Trump-supporters, such as you clearly are, have been thrilled tonight by comparing him to you. After all, you were a successful king bringing stability and prosperity to his people. You have pointed to that as vindication in the same way that President Trump points to a roaring economy as evidence of his administration's success. I ask you, then, do you think evangelical Trump supporters will be offended by your claims that the Bible's indictment of you is Fake News?

Jeroboam: Offended? Are you kidding me? These evangelical believers who are supportive of Trump are much more sophisticated than you give them credit for, Juan. With your question you betray yourself, showing that you think of evangelical Trump supporters in the same way Obama accidently betrayed himself on an open microphone, saying what he really felt, that Bible-belt buffoons cling to their guns and their religion.

Believers are more nuanced than that, Juan, despite Leftist views otherwise. All through the 2016 campaign the Dems basic message to evangelicals was, *"How can you support him? This man is not a deep student of this Bible you love so much."* What the media and Hillary supporters were actually saying, and evangelicals were not for a second fooled, is "we are going to use your simplistic idiocy against you. See! Listen to him as he says '*One Corinthians, Two Corinthians.*' You can't square your faith with this man who doesn't even know the proper way to reference the books of the Bible you love. He is so unlike you! However much you may agree with his policies, however much you may be excited by his promises, surely this is not your man. Stay with Hillary! She's a good Methodist, after all!"

Did that liberal strategy make any difference? Hell, no! Trump's supporters, both from evangelical and non-evangelical circles, support their president because, like I was, he is a fighter who cares nothing for the politically-correct language which led their country into the wilderness. He took his message straight to the people, nullifying the media's power, one Tweet at a time. I did exactly the same with far less tools at my disposal. I can't imagine how persuasive I would have been had I had Twitter in my day!

Juan, the Deep State just can't get over losing power. They wonder, "How can he thwart our every effort to depose him? We thought our attacks persuasive! We thought we'd had him so many times! With Russia and Mueller, with Stormy and Avenatti, with Manafort, Cohen, and Stone. What story will at last drag Trump off the throne?"

Trump is what conservative voters have been pleading for in their political leaders, someone who fights back, a leader who actually tries to deliver on their campaign promises. It is this that his supporters admire, his Bible knowledge, or lack thereof, notwithstanding. They are sick and tired of electing conservatives who, once in office, either govern as liberals or bend to pressure from the liberal media as if craving acceptance from a media that will always regard them as enemies. To the mainstream media John McCain and both Bushes were enemies, until they took positions against Trump, which magically rendered them as pure as Obama and Clinton, de-facto Democrats.

Now, to the prophet's recitation of Yeats. Was I a Rough Beast? Is Trump a Rough Beast? Here's my answer. Damn right! And that's what the people love about us, that we are strong enough to take the mantle and challenge the center when it shouldn't hold because it doesn't deserve to hold. Those "centers" of the Establishment Deep State in my day, by which I mean Solomon's temple and the Levitical priesthood, could not hold. Their undoing was my doing, and proudly so. Your president is fighting to show that today's centers of the Establishment Deep State can't and don't deserve, to hold. He was in a fight with a corrupt leadership within the DOJ and FBI, both of which were weaponized by Obama and Hillary, and has stepped out of the melee victorious. Takes a mighty Rough Beast to do that and sometimes, in the course of nations, a Rough Beast leader is necessary.

Yes, I was a Rough Beast, and I believe your president is as I was, a falcon soaring high enough to escape the ordinary orbit of politicians, no longer led by the madness of the Left's idiotic political-correctness. I love this reckless Rough Beast quality in your president. His voters sensed this about him from the beginning, which is why his brand grew through the primaries and the debates. Every sure-fire, Trump-ending revelation spouted by celebrity news anchors fell short of doing the job, even those embarrassing tapes of his lewd locker room talk about grabbing female genitalia. I have no doubt his supporters found those tapes embarrassing and repulsive but, at the end of the day, it didn't matter. They knew, when the time for voting came, who they were electing.

Shall they, then, be called hypocrites for standing by Trump? That's what you're really asking, Juan, isn't it? The answer is no. These conservative Trump supporters, regarded by the Establishment as Bible-toting idiots who would surely drop their support of such a vulgar candidate, were much smarter than they gave them credit for being, which is why those tapes did little to weaken his support. They knew they were voting for a president to lead the nation, not a pastor to lead a congregation.

And, I ask you, what president in the history of your country would you have wanted as a pastor? Jimmy Carter, perhaps? Hey, I'd love Jimmy as my Sunday School teacher. I'll wager he knows the Jeroboam story well, at least, in its official version. I hope President Carter is enjoying *The Five* today, gathering information for his next lesson. I like Carter, but look what a mess of malaise he left of the country, a situation which built the launching pad for another falcon, another Rough Beast named Reagan.

The Left, along with certain Never-Trumpers on the Right, thinking themselves enlightened, see President Trump and his supporters as deplorable. Hillary's letting that sentiment slip in the campaign with her *"basket of deplorables"* comment probably cost her the election. Thank God! Look, no matter how many apologies were forthcoming, voters knew instinctively that her words in that moment were likely the truest thing she had said in the entire campaign. That's exactly what she and her liberal colleagues think of conservative voters in the fly-over states.

I can only imagine how miserable she must have been while First Lady of Arkansas, pretending to respect the state her husband was born in and was governing.

C'mon. We all know that what she said is precisely what she and most of her supporters believed. Make no mistake, Trump-haters are also haters of Trump supporters, seeing them as simpletons clinging to their Bibles. That is the state of division existing in your country today. Mr. Trump didn't build those walls of division. Leftist ideas built those walls to the point that all Trump supporters are regarded by the Left as deplorable. Even wearing a red MAGA hat in public enflames the passions of a deranged lot which has lost its bearings. Why else would they have gone after that 16 year old kid from Covington without bothering to look deeper into the video? Because he was wearing a red hat with the letters, MAGA! That's all. Low hanging fruit for the deranged. The MAGA hat made him guilty, damn all facts to the contrary.

Look, after your country's globalist-minded leaders followed through on their apology tour, groveling in repentant sorrow for America on the world stage, only a Rough Beast of a president had a chance to get anything done. Weaker presidents, even those with genuinely conservative leanings, are simply not tough enough to stand up to a liberal media. I can't think of a single Republican in the 2016 primaries who wouldn't have wilted under the media's glare.

So yes, Rough Beast he is, and thankfully so, just as Rough Beast I was. I was a Rough Beast to the status quo dwelling in the swamp. The nation needed a Rough Beast to give us any chance at avoiding the economic collapse sure to follow if Solomon had kept spending a fortune on pet projects designed for his global audience rather than for the prosperity of his own people.

Ahijah may be surprised, but I know a little poetry as well, so let me offer my own bird imagery with a quote from William Blake:

The eagle never lost so much time

as when he submitted to learn of the crow.

I wasn't Yeats' falcon circling too high to listen to reason. I was Blake's eagle soaring high enough not to be distracted by the cawing of the crows below. And, Ahijah wasn't the falconer who let loose a monster. He was a crow seeking to crash a visionary.

I once saw a T-shirt from one of those hunters clinging to his guns in a southern, Trump-loving Red state. It said, "*I shot my coon dog for aimin' too low!*" Ahijah wanted me to aim low, by which I mean Jerusalem. But if I had kept Jerusalem as my people's pilgrimage site, my aim for real and lasting change would have been so low as to murder my own intentions to establish a new country, intentions he himself had planted into my heart.

The prophet contends I should have had faith and not fear. I say that neither faith nor fear played any role in my decision to forsake Jerusalem. It was common sense, a business decision utterly reasonable. That's what it was, and the positive results showed that it was the right decision. I was an eagle soaring.

Trump supporters love that he is an eagle soaring, despite the cawing of the Establishment and media crows who say, "*Stay down here with the Paris Climate Accords,"* "*Stay down here with Obamacare,"* "*Stay down here with the Iran Nuclear Deal,"* "*Stay down here with NAFTA,"* "*Stay down here with existing trade policies with China, no matter how one-sided and unfair."* "*Stay down here with a wall-less, open border."*

It's all too much "*Stay down here."* I say "*Hell no!"* to the crow. Let your eagle, President Donald J. Trump, fly higher than the crow's cawing, just as once the eagle who was Jeroboam ben Nebat soared higher that Ahijah's voice could reach.

CHAPTER EIGHT

Greg invites *The Five* to cast the movie, *"Jeroboam ben Nebat"*

Greg: Okay, enough, enough! When Yeats and Blake are being recited on *The Five* it's time for me to come to the rescue and offer a course correction. Queen Ano suggested we lighten up a moment ago, and I'm going to help us do just that.

Clearly our 3,000 year old guests are no strangers to political issues facing our country, including American culture and entertainment. We've already heard Jeroboam cast Jim Caviezel in the role of King Jeroboam in the film now certain to be made, since *The Five* has highlighted this incredibly ignored story. And what a great choice! I see the resemblance.

As all fans of *The Five* know, I'm not a religious person, but that's not to say I don't appreciate biblical drama. We have plenty of films about Bible stories of heroes like Moses and David. It's a shame this story isn't better known through the arts. Not to dramatize this story is like trying to tell American history without a mention of the Civil War. Imagine no books or movies about the Civil War! The Blue and the Gray, Red Badge of Courage, Gone with the Wind. The south may have lost, but they had their heroes, too, though Robert E. Lee statues are being torn down in today's supposed "wokeness." What we've learned today is that Jeroboam was a Robert E. Lee figure, admired by his contemporaries before being villainized later.

So, I want to ask each of our hosts a question. In the movie, "*Jeroboam ben Nebat*," which actor or actress would you cast for the role of the guest you've hosted today? This should be fun! Juan, I'll start with you. Who do you see playing Ahijah the prophet?

Juan: Wow, an interesting question, Greg. I'll give you two answers, since Ahijah's role covers so many years, he being a key figure at both ends of the Jeroboam story, separated by some twenty-five years.

I think that to play the prophet Ahijah in his early years I like Norman Reedus, who played Darryl on *The Walking Dead*. As I imagine that first scene outside Jerusalem, Ahijah's encounter with Jeroboam on the road, tearing his garment into twelve pieces and giving him ten in order to announce his astounding prophecy of Jeroboam's future political power, I see a disheveled prophet who is all action and few words, neither skilled in nor having any time for social courtesies. *Walking Dead* fans will agree that Reedus could pull that scene off in a compelling way. And, since our entire show tonight is an anachronistic dream, let me say that I can just imagine Darryl's Ahijah riding up to a startled Jeroboam on his motorcycle, hair flying in the wind.

Now, for the older, blind Ahijah who saw through Ano's attempt to deceive him, I offer a choice known for being politically conservative. Clint Eastwood plays the role of the crusty, irritable old man extremely well. Get ready to be impressed with my knowledge of the Bible. When Ahijah pronounced the horrible fate of the Jeroboam dynasty, he used a unique phrase to say that every male in the House of Jeroboam is doomed. He predicted that God would destroy everyone in the House of Jeroboam who "*urinates against the wall*," meaning, of course, every male. The King James Version used a word for "*urinate*" now considered a bit on the vulgar side, and I can hear Clint Eastwood delivering that line with all the necessary crudeness: "*I will cut off every one of the House of Jeroboam who pisseth against the wall*." I think Clint "*Go-ahead-make-my-day*" Eastwood would make the old man Ahijah come alive to modern audiences.

Greg: Great casting, Juan! Thank you for playing. What about you, Dana? Who would you cast in the role of the Queen Mother, Zeruah?

Dana: Remember, Greg, that her name is not Zeruah, but Zerlinda, the "*Beautiful Dawn*." I like for Zerlinda the Chilean-born actress Cote de Pablo, who played the Israeli, Ziva David on NCIS. Her name, Ziva, showing off my own Hebrew knowledge (actually, I just Googled it), means "*Radiance*," which seems not far from "*Beautiful Dawn*."

Ziva was radiant in that series. True, she's gorgeous, as is my guest, but Ziva's default setting was intelligence and a gritty toughness. Cote de Pablo in the Zerlinda role, I say. I can imagine her playing the widow, possessing the toughness needed to raise her child to be successful and powerful.

Greg: Again, I like it! Jedediah, you're pondering your answer now, I can see it. What say you as you cast the role of the beautiful Egyptian princess, Israel's Queen Ano?

Jedediah: You know, if Melania Trump were an actress and not a model, she'd be perfect. The parallels, as we have seen today in abundance, are uncanny between these foreign-born wives thrust into the role of First Lady of their countries.

To answer your question, I think I'd first offer the role of Ano to Jennifer Garner. Jennifer's big break came with the television series, *Alias*, in which she was a spy, a role requiring a certain mystique, which she pulled off admirably. Queen Ano needs someone able to portray all sides of her unique personality. There's the shy and retiring Ano of the Hebrew Bible who, as Juan has pointed out, never speaks. Then there's the intelligent and even jovial Ano whom we've seen on full display tonight. Jennifer Garner has all that, an actress intelligent, funny, sexy, and mischievous, all the qualities of Queen Ano we've delighted in tonight.

Now, you let Juan double up, so hold on. Just in case Jennifer turns down the role, let me offer a second choice, the immensely talented and politically conservative actress, Julienne Davis. She was interviewed on *Fox and Friends* recently about how conservatives in Hollywood are at a great disadvantage, how when she "came out" as a conservative she was shocked at how an industry that constantly talks about diversity is actually saturated with liberal group think. Julienne starred with

Tom Cruise as Mandy in the Stanley Kubrick film, *"Eyes Wide Shut,"* and I say that as a conservative she would be well-deserving of the role of Queen Ano. Let's face it, this is a film made for conservatives who would relish the opportunity to describe liberals as having their eyes wide shut to reality.

Greg: Fantastic! And what about you, Jesse? Who would you cast for King Jeroboam?

Jesse: It would be hard to improve on the king's choice of Jim Caviezel, who also is, I think, a Republican, but I'll give it a shot.

Who would I have star in this film as the wall-building, swamp-draining king from the Bible named Jeroboam ben Nebat? I'm not sure about his political views, but I would offer the role first to Chris Pine, who just last year starred in the film, *Outlaw King*. When Ahijah called Jeroboam a moment ago *"an outlaw of a king,"* it made me think of that film in which Chris plays Robert the Bruce who became King of Scots, coming to power to deliver long-denied justice to his people who were being heavily taxed and even conscripted by the king into fighting England's battles.

The roles are similar, so it seems perfect preparation for Chris to play Jeroboam, a leader who put his life on the line as he sought to end the unfairness of Solomon's conscription and taxation policies which funded his globalist aims. In fact (I just looked it up), Robert the Bruce was crowned king in 1306 and died in 1329, reigning for 23 years, just one more year than my new friend, King Jeroboam.

Greg: Chris Pine! Excellent choice! Hollywood, listen up! And now at last we come to Nebat, the father of Jeroboam seated by me. Since

Jesse and Jedediah are casting conservatives as a reward for being bold enough to stand up to the film industry's radical elements, I think for Nebat I'll name another conservative actor whose political views have cost him roles in liberal Hollywood, James Woods. I can imagine him drunk and spouting off to one of Solomon's soldiers and paying for that mistake with his life.

Dana: Wait Greg, that's not a good choice. Oops, I shouldn't have said that, should I? That's mean. Don't get me wrong, I love James Woods, but he's too old to play Nebat. Remember, Nebat died while a very young man, before his son was born. If James Woods gets the role, it needs to be a young James Woods. And, doesn't he usually play a villain?

Greg: Good points, Dana. But, what the hell, this is a dream anyway, so I cast for the role of Nebat a twenty-five year old James Woods. How's that? As for being a villain, he's a good conservative, so no way can he be a villain. Conservatives, like animals, are great.

So there you go, Hollywood! *Jeroboam ben Nebat* is a blockbuster in the making, and we've done your advance work. Get to it!

CHAPTER NINE

Dana Welcomes a Special Caller

Dana: That was a fun segment, Greg, but wait 'til America hears what's next. It will be even better. I was ready to ask our guests what they see as America's future, and we'll get to that, but we'll have to wait as we want first to hear from a very special caller. President Trump has been listening and has called in to join us on *The Five*.

Mr. President, I was watching when you unexpectedly called in to *Fox and Friends* a while back, just one of several examples of your impromptu media appearances. Thank you for watching us tonight sir, we are honored, and we welcome you to *The Five*.

President Trump: Thank you, Dana. I've been listening to your terrific show tonight with your very special guests. I wish we had known they were coming. Melania is watching the show with me and, had we known, we would have planned a State Dinner at the White House to welcome King Jeroboam, Queen Ano, and the entire family. Even Ahijah. Even you, Mr. Prophet, we would love to reach across the aisle and have you in the White House as well.

Jesse: Mr. President, your timing is perfect. You've heard us casting roles for the movie we're imagining. Who you would cast in the role of Donald Trump?

President Trump: Anybody, Jesse, except that despicable Alec Baldwin. I want someone playing me with a career on the way up, like the eagle King Jeroboam talked about, not someone like Baldwin who would better play the crow at this time when his career is sinking. Is that a good enough answer for you? Anybody but Alec.

Listen, I just wanted to call in to say how much I've enjoyed today's episode of The Five, and how much I've learned tonight about this fascinating story told in the Old Testament's books, One Kings and Two Kings.

Just kidding, by the way! I know it's First and Second Kings, but I can imagine already how *Fake News CNN*, no sense of humor at all, none, will grab what I just said and pretend I wasn't joking. It's one of their tricks they think gets by the people, but I tell you, it doesn't. The American people are much smarter than they give them credit for being, which is why CNN's ratings are in the toilet.

Jedediah: Mr. President, if I may step in to ask a question, you're catching a lot of flack for admitting you're a nationalist, as if that's a crime bequeathing you Hitlerian status. On the 100th anniversary of the Armistice ending World War 1, last November, President Macron of France was clearly aiming at you in speaking of nationalism as "old demons awakening." You, sir, like King Jeroboam, won in a populist movement. Isn't nationalism inherent, by definition, in a populist victory?

President Trump: It is, Jedediah, and I think every leader of their country should be a nationalist, even President Macron. He said nationalism is the opposite of patriotism, but that's just not true. Like Casey Stengel said, "*You can look it up!*" The dictionary definition of nationalism begins with a reference to patriotism.

Look, President Macron is coming at this from a globalist perspective and, frankly, was trying on the world stage to deflect attention from his own low popularity in France. As we all know now, President Macron, whom I like very much, set Paris to burning last year with riots caused by his idea to tax the peasants in order to pay for his globalist war on climate change.

I am a nationalist. I don't know if they had flags 3,000 years ago, but if so, I can't imagine King Jeroboam not standing in respect for his country's flag and for the many sacrifices made by those he called upon to keep that flag flying high.

So yes, I'm a proud nationalist, and a firm believer in American Exceptionalism, even though the media thinks these ideas somehow contain a racist, white supremist element. That's not how I use the word. People are smart. They hear me. The media tries hard to tag me with all those ugly labels, but they're not fooling anybody. The people know. My policies all flow from a nationalist core, and that has resulted in lifting all segments of the population, minorities especially, with record low unemployment and rising wages across every spectrum of our country.

Being a nationalist leader does not imply hatred for anybody or for any other country, despite media efforts to stain that word as if it belongs to the Nazis. I use the word to describe my love for our country's history and my passion for its future. That's all. So yes, thanks for the question, Jedediah. I am proud to be a nationalist.

Greg: Mr. President, welcome to *The Five* and thank you for calling. I've often said on this show that yours is the most transparent presidency in history, and your call and openness to answer questions in a spur-of-the-moment way is another example of why I say that.

Sir, of all the comparisons with King Jeroboam which have been made tonight, the "Wall" is the most fascinating to me. He had more success in getting Jeroboam's Wall done than you've had. Where are we with Trump's Wall?

President Trump: Well, let's remember that his wall was a lot smaller and a lot less expensive, a "virtual" wall, as you have said. Thank you for that question, Greg. I've listened with fascination about how King Jeroboam, in a tough act after he became king, built his wall. I admire toughness and I assure you, it will take toughness to get the wall built in the current political climate. You know that. We have a crisis on our southern border that the Democrats are unwilling to acknowledge or address. That must change for the security of the United States. It must change.

Remember, though, that Jeroboam's Wall was built to keep people in, to keep them home. My wall, of course, is being built for an opposite purpose, to stem the tide of illegal immigration, a crisis because of weak and stupid laws from previous administrations and from a weak

Congress pandering to political correctness, the opposite of the kind of toughness needed to make difficult decisions.

So, while it's interesting to connect Trump's Wall with Jeroboam's Wall, it seems to me that a better analogy to Jeroboam's virtual wall would be the "virtual" wall of my economic policies which have stemmed the flow of American companies leaving our borders. My economic wall was built with smart, commonsense policies designed to keep industries and jobs at home where they belong.

Bottom line, though, Jeroboam's Wall had the same goal as mine, to fulfill our pledge to keep our people safe and prosperous, a national leader's highest priority. It's what Solomon forgot, evidently, though I admit I had no idea about that until tonight. I'm no Bible scholar, but everyone knows the name Solomon, right? You hear Solomon's name and immediately think of a king who was wise and wealthy. Before tonight, I would have preferred being compared to him than to Jeroboam.

Not so, though, after this episode of *The Five*. Who knew the name Jeroboam? You'd have to be a pretty serious Bible student to know his story, but I think he's made a convincing case that he, not Solomon, was the truly wise leader, a nationalist passionate about his country and working hard to make the lives of his people better.

Obviously, I can relate to the problem of a media offering Fake News. The king has enlightened us all tonight as to how the Bible's historians did to him what the mainstream media is trying to do to me.

Amazing how Solomon did so little for the people and yet got all the glory. Sound familiar? The Solomon we learned about this evening was a globalist who brought so much misery to his people that they revolted, making Jeroboam king. Solomon must have had a fantastic PR team, clearly the recipient of vast amounts of positive press from the Establishment media, something neither Jeroboam nor I have enjoyed. To say the obvious, virtually all mainstream press reporting on my administration has been unfairly negative.

That's especially true, of course, when it comes to the wall on our southern border, a topic on which the Left has lost its mind, reversing their own statements made during the Clinton and Obama administrations during which, if you listen to their news conferences from those days, they said the exact same things I'm saying now. But today's Democrats have been pulled out to the fringes on the far Left, having to abandon their own words and follow Pelosi in declaring the wall immoral.

It's not immoral, it's common sense, and I intend to get that wall built despite the Democrat's resistance in Congress. It's a national emergency. It must be done. Border security is vital for our future, and I won't let congressional weakness and inaction sacrifice our future anymore that King Jeroboam would have let the words of the prophets sacrifice the future of his country by allowing policies that would have drained his country's resources.

Juan: Mr. President, you told minorities in the campaign, "*What the hell do have to lose?*"

Greg: Oh, what a shameless plug for your book, Juan!

Juan: No, seriously, my question Mr. President is, don't you think that your campaign statement to blacks and minorities, "*What the hell* *do you have to lose?"* is a way to enflame racial tensions and erase the progress of those who worked so hard for civil rights in America?

President Trump: No Juan, I don't think so at all. I was saying the obvious, that as a voting bloc the Democrats have depended upon for decades, what has been accomplished by voting Democrats into power?

It sounds to me like Jeroboam had the same message to those leaders of the ten tribes who were reluctant to follow him, those who feared distancing themselves from the status quo. Sounds like he said, "What have you got to lose? Your sons are being conscripted into Solomon's labor force, being made to leave their homes and their families. He's using you!"

Mine is a similar message to minorities. What has your allegiance to the Democrats for these many decades done for you? It's time to try something else. And, I've been proven right with that message. With record low black and Hispanic unemployment, I suggest that those minorities who are coming over to the Republican party and conservative governance are seeing the rewards of their boldness.

This is the same message offered by every leader who emerges from outside the Establishment. I saw the film Jesse referred to a few minutes ago, *Outlaw King*. I love the story of Robert the Bruce, and I recall in the film how he offered exactly that message to the tribes in Scotland who at first were reluctant to embrace him as king, fearing the consequences should the revolt end with failure. "What have you got to lose?" was Robert the Bruce's message, too. Look, it takes guts to answer that question and to risk change, but enough were bold to make

Robert the Bruce's movement a success. The same is true of Jeroboam and of Trump.

Dana: Mr. President, as a president who is clearly a supporter of Israel, following an Obama administration which seemed to distance itself from Israel, how has our show tonight strengthened or weakened your stance?

President Trump: Great question, Dana. I've been an unapologetic supporter of Israel and tonight's visit with King Jeroboam strengthens my commitment. As you know, I alone stood for doing what every recent president knew was right, said was right, yet failed to accomplish. I moved our embassy to Jerusalem.

Honestly, one of the things that has mystified me is American Jewish support for a Left which has clearly embraced anti-Semitic voices like Louis Farrakhan and Marc Lamont Hill, who in a United Nations speech last year called for a free Palestine, *"from the river to the sea,"* a well-known phrase calling for the extermination of Israel. CNN did finally fire him for that, but only after intense pressure was brought to bear.

Listen, I don't want to hijack your excellent show. I just wanted to call and thank *The Five* for bringing out the Jeroboam/Trump comparisons, businessmen both of us who became strong leaders of prosperous nations, despite having to weather being treated unfairly and viciously by the Deep State Establishment. Your viewers today have heard, not only comparisons between King Jeroboam and myself, nationalists building walls leading to security and prosperity, but also the Obama/Solomon comparisons as globalists concerned with their reputations abroad, and the Hillary/Rehoboam comparisons as weak potential successors to their globalist predecessors. Your show has been wonderful.

Oh, and Melania absolutely loves the comparisons of her that have been made tonight with Queen Ano. Queen Ano has clearly been the biggest hit on *The Five* tonight, as is always First Lady Melania in the White House and wherever she goes. I wish they could meet.

Dana: I'm sure we can try to get that done, Mr. President, as I doubt that our guests have any other engagements to hurry off to attend, ours being a world exclusive. I wonder, sir, if before you go you might have any questions for our special guests?

President Trump: Thank you, I do have one, Dana. My question is for Nebat, the king's father. While you were respected and successful, it was your son whose accomplishments assured that your name would live forever. Dying young, you missed his life, all the opportunities to be involved as a father, to express your pride in his achievements. Still, from the vantage point of the great Beyond, you've obviously watched over your son's life. So, Nebat, my question is this. What did you feel most, looking down on your son as he led Israel? Was it anger at fate for missing his life? Was it sorrow due to your absence? Was it pride and joy in his accomplishments? As you know, my father has long been departed from us, but I wonder what he feels as sees what I have become.

Nebat: Good evening, Mr. President. I am humbled, indeed, by your call and that you would direct a question to me. I felt no anger at fate, Mr. President. Death removes anger. I did possess pride and joy in abundance as I watched my son's life.

Still, I think that what I felt most is something you did not mention. Watching his rise to power, watching his love for his people and how much he gave of himself to better their lives, all while enduring virtually universal condemnation by a press, by prophets and scribes who really had no idea who my son was, I felt what I'll describe as gratitude. I was filled with gratitude to God for the blessing of having fathered such a son who was willing to endure what he endured in order to serve. He was willing to endure so much abuse, and none of it necessary. He could have gone back to Egypt at any time to live out his days in abundance, but he chose to suffer as he served. For my son, Jeroboam ben Nebat, I say *Baruch ha-Shem*. Blessed be the Name.

President Trump: Thank you for your answer, sir. What a fascinating show tonight, and I congratulate *The Five*. Thanks for allowing me some time, and now I'll let you get back to your show.

CHAPTER TEN

Jesse confronts King Jeroboam with the odd story of 1 Kings 13

Jesse: What a great segment, Dana. President Trump obviously feels the connection with Jeroboam which "*The Five*" has highlighted tonight, a biblical example of how Fake News can impact a leader's legacy.

Now, as we come back to our panel, I have a question for my guest, King Jeroboam. While we've talked about most of the biblical narrative of your life and political career, especially focusing on the 1 Kings narrative, there's one large chunk of that narrative we've skipped over entirely.

Jeroboam: Yes, I'm aware. And, I suppose you're going to bring it up?

Jesse: I am. Since it's been a recurring theme here tonight, let me say that we've talked much about both the Dawn and the Dusk of your reign, as the Bible relates it. Your ascent to power from outside the Establishment is told in Chapter 12, and the story of your son's death and a brief epitaph of your own life is told two chapters later, in Chapter 14. We've covered all of that, your Dawn and your Dusk.

What have we missed? Well, in-between those two chapters is 1 Kings 13, a long and convoluted story not yet mentioned around our table of Ten. It's an ugly story shining a spotlight on a weak moment for you, and clearly revealing how the authors wanted to paint your legacy. Not a story from either your Dawn or your Dusk, this story is high noon in your life, a blazing sun casting a verdict on your reign. And, sir, it's not pretty.

It tells of an event just after you set up your altar, your wall, in Bethel near your southern border. Wasting no time, the passage begins on a highly critical note for how you arbitrarily set up your own religious calendar, your own feast days, totally ignoring Hebrew traditions, and then came to Bethel to offer sacrifice on one of your new holidays.

What it describes is an unnamed prophet who had come up from Judah, in the south, intent on causing a disturbance. He interrupts you in the middle of your ritual, crying loudly as if addressing the altar itself. *"O Altar, Altar! A child shall be born in the House of David, Josiah by name."* He goes on to prophesy to the altar, as if you weren't even worthy to be addressed, that this future King Josiah would one day tear it down, that your precious wall keeping the Israelites from making pilgrimage to Jerusalem would be defiled and erased from history.

The story is just beginning, so stay with me. It says you were so angry at this rude interruption that you stretched out your hand to command your guards to seize the prophet. When your hand was outstretched, it withered and became paralyzed. This frightened you so much that you begged the prophet for mercy. Mercy was given, so that you immediately regained the use of your hand.

It must have seemed like magic. Stunned, but thankful for the removal of God's judgment, the text says you invited this prophet to the palace to eat and to receive a reward. He refused, saying God had instructed him not to eat or drink until he was back home in Judah.

Now, if our viewers think that's odd, the story becomes even more bizarre. One of the local prophets from Bethel, hearing of the disturbance, chased down this southern prophet and found him on the road. Inviting him home to eat and drink, the prophet again insisted that he could not, because the Lord had commanded him to go directly home to Judah without taking refreshment. That's when the local prophet, claiming his own prophetic credentials, lied. Outright lied. He told the southern prophet that the Lord himself had rescinded his word, and sent him as a messenger to tell the prophet to eat before he traveled home.

I know, it's a long story. Stay with me, it's almost over. The prophet from the south believed the lie spoken by the northern prophet and so went to eat at his home. While eating, the lying prophet from the north received a true word from the Lord, prophesying now to the southern prophet that, because he had been disobedient, he would never make it home, he would never be buried in his family's grave. And, sure enough, on the way home, a lion met this southern prophet on the road and mauled him to death.

The lying prophet from Bethel, now consumed with guilt that his lie had caused this prophet's death, took the corpse and buried it, proclaiming now that the southern prophet was his "*brother*," and telling his sons, "*When I die, lay my remains beside his.*"

That's the end of 1 Kings 13, but to hear the true end of the story we have to forward 300 years to 630 B. C., during the reign of King Josiah as told in 2 Kings 22. Your northern kingdom of Israel had already been extinct for nearly a century when the reformer king, Josiah, did exactly as was predicted. When the bones of these two prophets were found, King Josiah, respecting those long dead prophet brothers, one from the north and one from the south, commanded that their bones not be disturbed.

End of the story. Care to comment?

Jeroboam: Well, Jesse, it looks like you've laid a trap for me and you've caught me. I'm afraid now I'll have to take back all the good things I said about you earlier.

Not! I'm only kidding. Look, could there be any more convincing proof of the historical bias of the text than this silly story? Just as President Trump called parts of the Mueller Report which portrayed him in a bad light "bullshit," that's what I say about 1 Kings 13. This chapter, which you've struggled to summarize due to its length and complexity, is nothing more than an effort to stain the legacy of my successful reign of 22 years. This is pure fabrication dreamed up in the bogus "witch hunt" of southern historians from Judah who, long after I was dead and buried, still sought to demonize me.

More than any other story in the Bible, this story reeks of *Jeroboam Derangement Syndrome.* Don't you get it? The story, in sum, teaches that the northern prophets, my prophets in Israel, are all liars who will at last come to their senses and realize that the southern prophets are forever their brothers, their bones to be laid side-by-side for all eternity so that these brothers are now at last together, the guilty forgiven and the innocent forgiving.

But as for Jeroboam, who caused it all? Well, *mene mene tekel upharsin,* a Hebrew phrase meaning, "*You have been weighed in the balances and found wanting.*" I am the only one condemned, the *Unheilsherrscher,* the Unholy King. Even my prophet, that lying prophet, is forgiven. I alone remain guilty, my sin unforgivable.

Those two prophets in this story, Jesse, are made up. Total fiction. They are invented by the authors to be representatives of two nations. The northern prophet represented the entire two hundred year span of my kingdom of Israel. The authors, writing this long after Ephraim was no more, concocted this story to teach that the nation could now, at last, be one, as it once had been under David and Solomon. The curse of Jeroboam ben Nebat and his wall had now forever been removed, so that the warring brothers could be reunited.

What rubbish! If there's a semblance of truth here it is that, sure, we had the occasional protestor on my official visits to the altar, especially in the early days. It's true that I changed the calendar and our holidays. That's what new nations do, right? They change the calendar. I suspect when your southern states left the Union they didn't celebrate July 4th as Independence Day, either.

It's also true that we had hecklers. They were rare but they did pop up from time to time. Think of it like the disruption of your conservative leaders while eating at restaurants or in other public places. It's an embarrassment, that's what it is, but nothing we couldn't handle. I don't think the Left realizes, even today, how the common man is put off by this kind of irrationality.

My God, you've got Democrat leaders calling for followers to get in the faces of well-known conservatives whom they might accidently encounter in public. It's more than an embarrassment. It's shameful and it's despicable.

Jesse, this is Fake News. My hand never withered. No heckler was ever sent an invitation to dine in the palace. How stupid would that be! And I know of no prophet ever killed by a lion after confronting me and, believe me, I had plenty of prophets confront me. It's Fake News, Jesse, pure nonsense generated by southern historians 300 years after I lived, a tale spun strait from the PR arm of King Josiah's government. If Josiah was a reformer as history says, he was also, no doubt, a superb marketer.

C'mon, do you really believe that a prophet 300 years before Josiah was born actually used his name in my presence to predict the altar's destruction? Good grief, give me a break! Believe that if you will, but doesn't it make more sense that his name was written in by later historians wishing to bolster their king's credentials, while further obliterating my own?

Jesse: Your majesty, if I may, one more question about this story. While the prophet is unnamed in 1 Kings 13, there is a tradition from the Talmud and from Josephus, as well as others, that this prophet was none other than Iddo the Seer, whose anti-Jeroboam writings are talked about in the biblical book of 2 Chronicles.

Jeroboam: Ah, yes, Iddo. He was indeed a prophet in my time who wrote about me negatively, a Jim Acosta figure, if you will. Or better, Michael Avenatti, who was loved by the mainstream media as the slayer of Trump. For a while, until he proved to be a dishonest fraud. CNN would have hired Iddo, no doubt, this grabber of the microphone, this embarrassment to his profession.

Jessie, I never had the privilege of meeting Iddo the Seer, but I did know something of his reputation. If he were around today, I'd call him *Guido Iddo*, a Rasputin kind of character, a mystic, a self-proclaimed holy man. Just really a weird guy, perfect for this weird story.

But let's face it, no one would know the name Iddo except for me. I made him, in addition to an entire class of anti-Jeroboam prophets, including our own Ahijah sitting at this table of ten tonight. These prophets would have no lasting legacy were it not for Jeroboam ben Nebat. I made them! If they saw me as an *Unheilsherrscher*, at least I gave them something to preach and write about. They all sang in the same choir and their favorite anthem was, *"O Felix Culpa!" "O Happy Fault"* of Jeroboam, that has given me a voice to be remembered, a glorious legacy of resistance.

The same choir sings today, by the way, its most accomplished voices ranging from the soprano sounds of *MSNBC* to the bass notes sounded by *The New York Times*. In between are the tenor sounds of *CNN* and the alto voices of *The Huffington Post*. Of Trump they sing, *"O Felix Culpa!" "O Happy Fault"* that increased our subscriptions and upped our ratings and kept our employees working. Without him, where would we be? *O Felix Culpa!*

You know what I think is really going on in this passage, Jesse? By presenting a picture of me as panicking with a paralyzed hand, it seeks to describe my administration as being in constant panic mode. You see the same thing today with Trump, nothing delighting liberals more than describing Trump's White House as in total chaos. There will always be palace intrigue, of course, but I suspect most of those accounts are wildly exaggerated and, without question, told with a hidden agenda. How many times has the media imagined that their magic had "withered" the hand of the president? "He's done for!" they think. "Surely this time he's done for!"

That's what 1 Kings 13 is, Fake News to make me look weak and my administration in crisis. Look, like every political leader in history, we had serious challenges to confront, hard decisions to make, and differences of opinion among my advisors. I'm sure that, from day to day, our palace seemed in chaos. I would tell my advisors, when they became worried, something like what your president told the world on New Year's Day 2019, *"Calm down and enjoy the ride! Good things are happening."* Your president seems not to mind the roller coaster thrill, nor did I. I fired many, sent them home, though in my day they didn't write too many tell-all books afterwards, if you know what I mean.

In the last verse of this ugly chapter, southern historians from Judah fix my legacy the way they wanted it to be read. The summary following this puerile story proves the bias of the entire narrative: *"Even after this, Jeroboam did not change his evil ways, but once more appointed priests for the high places from all sorts of people. Anyone who wanted to become a priest he consecrated for the high places. This was the sin of the house of Jeroboam that led to its downfall and to its destruction from the face of the earth."*

Put simply, they were angry that I was draining the swamp, successfully giving opportunity to a wider range of individuals. That's all. Had the House of Jeroboam outlasted the House of David, you and your ancestors would have heard a very different story of the lives of Solomon and Jeroboam. Future generations would have seen my actions as progressive, expanding opportunity and diversity. Wouldn't anti-Trump liberals be all for that?

You know, Jesse, blinded by Jeroboam-hatred, what they did to me by destroying my good reputation was criminal. The same is true today. How many times have false narratives been embraced by the media if the slightest chance presents itself that they might twist a story to be critical of the president and his supporters? From Judge Kavanaugh to the Covington Kids to Jussie Smollett and so many more stories. It would be comical were it not so serious. I think, though, if the world were to come to its senses and cases ever brought to court, all they would need to do is claim *Jeroboam Derangement Syndrome* as their legal defense, just as today's criminal press could do with *Trump Derangement Syndrome*. It's a real thing, and could mount a successful legal defense. *"I'm sick. I couldn't help myself."* There would be enough evidence, I think, to acquit.

CHAPTER ELEVEN

Jedediah polls the panel on Trump's re-election chances

———

Jedediah: Well, I have to ask our guests. Since we're coming close to the 2020 election, do you think Trump will be re-elected? Let's start with you, Nebat. Trump's chances in 2020?

Nebat: I hate to say it, but I think that no, Mr. Trump will not be re-elected. His campaign offered two centerpiece promises, and those were the reasons he was elected. He promised to nominate conservative judges, especially should Supreme Court openings occur, but also throughout the judicial system. This he has done in abundance.

His second major promise was to build the wall, and that, of course, has led to a different result. He has not been able to build the wall on his own terms and in his own timing, and that has led to, well, just a mess with government shutdowns and more. That, in my opinion, will do him in.

That said, I think his four years have been wonderful for the United States, and that his impact will be felt for decades to come, much to the chagrin of the Left.

Jedediah: What about you, Zerlinda?

Zerlinda: I agree with my husband. He will, sadly, not be re-elected. The media, as well as areas of government that have been weaponized against him, especially the corrupt leadership of the FBI will, at the end of the day, prevail. I can't imagine the storm that man is having to weather from a media out to destroy him.

Jedediah: King Jeroboam? What think you?

Jeroboam: I disagree with my mother and my father. Absolutely President Trump will be re-elected, I have no doubt, whatsoever. Sleepy Joe and Crazy Bernie won't stand a chance, particularly if the economy continues to hum. That new Attorney General, Mr. Barr, will uncover a corruption within the former administration that far exceeds the crimes of Watergate, they knowingly using Fake News paid for by the DNC and Hillary, as premise to spy on the Republican nominee's campaign. Look, the Democratic candidates are being pulled to the radical Left, embracing policies the American people will never stomach, gifting your president with the 2020 election so that he can continue to build his legacy of commonsense policies creating economic growth.

Speaking of the economy, those new stars of the Left, most notably that moron, Ocasio-Cortez, have created a dumpster fire among the Democrats that Speaker Pelosi will have a hard time getting under control. Her *Green New Deal* logically leads to the elimination of air travel and cruises and autos, all in the name of this new religion of climate change before which all are asked to bow and make sacrifice. I saw her myself say the world will end in twelve years if things don't happen now, and I hear now that Beto shortened that estimate to ten. These people need a serious psychological evaluation as they breathlessly offer Climate Change's Apocalypse du jour, the latest addition to the Boom in Doom that has always been the charming allure of eschatological studies. The good news for Trump is that these rising stars of the Left do not offer a winning message in 2020. Sensible Dems know that, of course. Add to that dismal economic message how that Muslim woman from Minnesota, Omar, is throwing gasoline on the dumpster fire with blatant anti-Semitism and anti-American ignorance.

Mother is right, in one way, of course. The media will seek in every way they can to stain Trump's legacy in an unrepairable way. They did so successfully in my case, which is why what your viewers today are hearing, my side of the story, is being heard for the first time. They, the press, the Bible's chroniclers, muzzled me with no avenue to get my message to the people. That is, until today, until *The Five*.

I think, though, and this is the good news for the president, he won't have to wait 3,000 years to tell his story. Modern technology makes it easy for him to challenge his challengers in a way I could not. Today's media simply cannot get away with tactics that once were unassailable, as you have seen repeatedly in recent years. The internet has given conservative fact-checkers all they need to debunk the Fake

News offered by the liberal media, going back to Dan Rather's blatant attempt to smear a president with Fake News.

Trump will win in 2020, Jedediah, and continue to build a legacy which, at the end of the day, will not be dismantled by the liberal media in the same way the southern scribes destroyed the public's ability to see and remember my positive achievements. Jedediah, your president, Donald J. Trump, deserves to be re-elected, and he will be.

Jedediah: And what about you, Mr. Prophet? Will President Trump survive his re-election bid?

Ahijah: I will only say that for the good of the country and the world, I hope not. However, I fear that Jeroboam is right. He will be re-elected, and just as Jeroboam's ten tribes became the famous "lost" ten tribes, Trump will continue to lead America on a path toward becoming irrecoverably lost. The king is correct that the party's ideological drift to the far Left will have taken a heavy toll by the time November 2020 arrives.

Jedediah: And now, finally, Queen Ano? What about Trump 2020?

Ano: I think that he will not be re-elected, Jedediah. And I think this may be good for him, for I see in him something that I saw in my husband. He is a good man, and while it may seem that he weathers well the media's persistent attacks, I remember how my husband was deeply hurt, in a way no one else could see, in a way he would never admit. So many of the things they said about him simply weren't true. For his own sake, I hope he's not re-elected.

Political life takes a toll on the family. It did for me. I never felt accepted, especially for my being Egyptian. I can only imagine, in your world of social media and constant news coverage, how intense the pressure must be on your First Lady, with whom I feel kinship.

CHAPTER TWELVE

Dana Asks, "Is America near its dusk?"

Dana: Thank you, Queen Ano, for pointing out the personal costs that our political leaders, along with their families, pay for being in the spotlight 24-7.

I want now to ask each of our guests, not just where you see President Trump's future after 2020, whether in the White House or back at Trump Tower, but a more existential question. I want to ask where do you see America's future should we continue down this path? With a 3,000 year history of observing world events, I think your insight might be valuable.

The *Dawn* and *Dusk* theme has been with us all evening, so I'll frame my question with that motif. Our country has been a shining light of freedom in the world, not just for a single day of 24 hours, but for over 24 centuries. Is America's light fading? Is the long American day coming to an end? Zerlinda, you of the *"Beautiful Dawn,"* I'll start with you. What do you think?

Zerlinda: I think, Dana, that America's light will continue to shine bright. I see no dusk ahead for America, at least not in the way you intend by your question, as if the America you have known all your life is coming to an end.

Dawn and dusk, you see, should not be spoken of as a single event. In life as in nature, it's a cycle, a continuous spiral into the future, something like a slow-moving wormhole. Every country, every people, endure many dawns and many dusks. My country of Israel is no exception. Indeed, it is perhaps the best of all examples.

Conservatives were shocked when your President Obama promised to "fundamentally transform America." They shouldn't have been. Transformation is always necessary and, I believe, guided by a divine hand.

The main reason, Dana, that I have confidence in the surviving and the thriving of your Republic is based on my firm belief in divine providence. Divine providence created Israel and has sustained it through the millennia, including many bright dawns from Abraham in ancient history to Zionism in modern history. We've also experienced many dark moments when it looked as if the light was forever extinguished, such as the Babylonian and Roman destructions of the temple on the 9th of Av in ancient history, and the horrors of the Holocaust in modern history.

Dawns and dusks there will surely be, turnings of divine providence but, as the psalmist sang, the believer in providence can sing, *"from the rising of the sun to its setting, the Name of the LORD is to be praised."*

I believe that the same turning of divine providence which created and sustained Israel also brought about the creation of the United States of America, and will sustain it. I am a firm believer in American Exceptionalism, convinced that God's unique blessings rest upon this great land, despite any setbacks which people may wrongly regard as the sun setting on America's greatness. Goodness, is the present time more calamitous than fifty years ago, when the 60s witnessed assassinations and cultural upheaval? Yet, America not only survived, but thrived. And, surely America felt itself close to dusk a hundred years before, during the Civil War.

Yet, for all that, America has not yet come close to the agony of the Jews who went into Babylonian captivity after Solomon's temple was destroyed in 586 B. C. Still, as dark as that captivity was, when the people by the rivers of Babylon sat down by the willows to weep, mourning as they remembered Zion, they refused to forget.

"If I forget you, Jerusalem, may my right hand wither," they said. That, by the way, is the real reason behind the writing of the Fake News story you just talked about, my son's hand withering as he offered sacrifice in Bethel. He had turned his back on Jerusalem and so his hand withered. Get it? Surely you get it! That was the point of whoever wrote the story. It's not that difficult. What is the current sarcastic way to remind people of the obvious? I think, "Keep up, people!"

Look, in dark times, Jewish determination to remember was more than the remembering of a building, even a building as glorious as Solomon's temple. No, rather they were remembering who they were as a people chosen by God. This brought them to the dawn of a new age, liberating God from a building and forever eliminating the need for pilgrimage to any sacred site. Not to Jerusalem, not to Dan, not to Bethel. God was with them, no matter on which side of the wall they were, whatever wall, wherever the diaspora took them.

The Babylonian Captivity, as terrible a dusk as it was for the Jewish people, was the dawn of a new and better age in which animal sacrifices, the bloody mess of Jerusalem' temple, were no more. People learned through hard experience that God's absence offered a deep and mysterious essence of divine presence. The essence of God's presence everywhere was the absence of God's presence in the temple. The Divine One no longer was imagined as seated in the Holy of holies in Jerusalem. Perhaps my son figured that out long before the rest of us.

I have every confidence, Dana, that America was, is, and will be a bright and shining light for the world, a beacon of hope in a world dreary lighted.

Dana: Thank you, Zerlinda, for a beautiful answer resting on the hope of divine providence. Ahijah, I turn next to you. America's future?

Ahijah: Dana, I hear many screams about constitutional crisis, but I see no such thing, even as opposed to Trump as I am. The media and the Democrats are crying wolf in the most benign of situations, seeing a racist under every MAGA hat. From those poor Covington kids caught up in a frenzy of misplaced wrath to that Chicago actor named Jussie paying his own attackers to wear the gear of supposed Trumpian racism as they pretended to assault him, the media's obsession with

Trump-hatred makes them susceptible to great error, rushing to judgment before facts are known and, well, looking stupid when the facts come out, not to mention, liable. This is horrible, because there are real hate crimes out there, and when the real thing arises, they will have lost their power to stir the people to caring. No prophet is worth much with voice muted.

I agree with Zerlinda in seeing divine providence at work. But, in this I beg to differ. She mentioned not needing to go on pilgrimage. Let me say that I think that the way for America to shine again with that light which has illuminated so much of the world for two centuries is for the entire country to go on pilgrimage. Americans need to experience a sacred journey, as did our tribes in the long-ago past. I don't mean that literally, of course. The country is far too big and the people far too many. I mean, rather, that the country needs to experience the spirit of pilgrimage as a rediscovery of who they are.

Let me explain. The Jeroboam story has pilgrimage as a central component. Jerusalem? Dan? Bethel? The wall, as you have called his altar, was all about pilgrimage. Israel needed pilgrimage to survive as a people, a sacred journey to remind them who they are and what they are called to be. In this, Jeroboam ben Nebat understood the truth that it was a national emergency. Pilgrimage, the means of re-discovering who we are, was needed then, and is equally needed today.

Pilgrimage is fundamentally different from what you call vacation, which is usually travel in search of pleasure. The pilgrim's quest is for enlightenment. To make pilgrimage implies, not treating yourself to an exotic destination to experience pleasure or to view beauty or simply to relax. Pilgrimage requires giving up something of oneself, offering one's heart up to something higher than themselves. The heart of the pilgrim's experience is to give up one's uniqueness to become part of a larger community.

It is that which America is losing, a spirit of community, and I think the only way to regain it is pilgrimage. I would advise the Democrats, whom I generally support, to soften their focus on Identity Politics. The tribalism caused by that focus is the reverse of pilgrimage and can only damage the country.

To me, the most beautiful portion of the Hebrew Bible is called the Psalms of Ascent, fifteen songs from Psalm 120 – 134. My favorite is Psalm 122:

I was glad when they said unto me,

"Let us go to the house of the LORD!"

Our feet are standing

within your gates, O Jerusalem!

Jerusalem – built as a city

That is bound firmly together.

To it the tribes go up,

The tribes of the LORD,

As was decreed for Israel,

To give thanks to the Name of the LORD.

Sha'alu shalom Yerushalayim!

(Pray for the peace of Jerusalem!)

Notice that though it is the individual who receives the invitation to pilgrimage, "*I . . . was glad when they said to . . . ME,*" it is to a larger community that the pilgrim is invited to join. It is not, as some eastern religions might imagine, a private climbing of the mountain in a quest to find a guru who can led one person at a time to understand who they are in relation to deeper truths.

No, but true pilgrimage is communal, which is why the passage shifts so abruptly from singular to plural, "*Let US go up. OUR feet are standing within your gates. The TRIBES go up.*" These psalms weren't intended to be solos. The Songs of Ascent were sung, chanted, or recited by the community, drawing those who had inconvenienced themselves for the journey into an awareness of who they were as a community. I have made my dislike for President Trump clear tonight, but I must say that his "Salute to America" on July 4th at the National Mall was exquisite, a rehearsal of the nation's history that became a pilgrimage moment for those who endured the rain and discomfort.

America celebrates a constitution that allows individuals to rise. That is wonderful! It is the American Dream. But how can the American Dream endure without a communal sense of who you are as a people? This is what you are losing in such a fractured time, and you cannot blame that on Donald Trump. I wish it were that easy, but truth is never easy.

So, my prescription for a fractured America is that you go on a pilgrimage. A virtual pilgrimage, of course. To where? Not to New York as the center of your commerce, nor Washington D. C. as the center of your government, nor certainly Hollywood and Disneyworld as the center of your entertainment.

I say let America take a virtual pilgrimage to Philadelphia, the city of brotherly love. There, where it all started in Independence Hall on July 4, 1776. *"Let US go up,"* so that you can say, *"OUR feet are standing"* in Independence Hall, there made to remember who you are and what you are called to be. Let the crack in the Liberty Bell remind you of your nation's unity despite how bent and broken you are. And, with that bell in your imagination, remember the words of T. S. Eliot:

> *We will not cease from exploration*
> *And the end of all our exploring*
> *Will be to arrive where we started,*
> *And know the place for the first time.*

Dana: A beautifully poetic answer from our prophet. Thank you, Ahijah of Shiloh. Now, what about you, King Jeroboam. Where do you see America headed?

Jeroboam: I disagree entirely. America doesn't need pilgrimage, all due respect to the prophet. Pilgrimage is a call to look backward to discover the roots of community. I admit the benefit of it, of course. I built my kingdom by addressing the tribal need for pilgrimage to solidify the national community. So, yes, it's vital, but it's also secondary.

Which is why I offer the very opposite advice as that given by the prophet. You must move forward, not backward, and you do that by emphasizing, not the community over the individual, but the individual over the community. In other words, the capitalist dream is more important to the nation than socialism.

When I speak of the individual over the community, I don't mean that in selfish way. The fact is, the more the individual prospers, the more the community prospers. That's America's glory, establishing and preserving the rights and the opportunities of each individual to live fully into their potential.

Like your president, I prefer to call us forward. Just as he did in his 2019 State of the Union address, I called upon my people to "*Choose Greatness.*" That, by the way, I regard as Mr. Trump's "Moses" Moment, which is so much better than Mr. Booker's "Spartacus" Moment! Moses told the people, "*I set before you life and death, blessing and cursing. Choose Life!*"

So, in answer to your question, Dana, I see America responding to that call and moving toward evermore greatness. *Make America Great Again* was a great motto, having an element of pilgrimage infused in it, the word "again" suggesting a remembering of America's beginnings.

I like "*Choose Greatness*" even more for his 2020 Campaign, a clarion call to move forward, as was my motto, *May the People be Great.* No need for the word "*Again.*" "*Choose Greatness*" says it better. We weren't looking back, but forward, as is your president. You need no pilgrimage to the past, Mr. President, your pledge to move forward is enough.

As unpopular with the mainstream media and Establishment politicians as he is today, monuments will one day be made to your president, just as there are now monuments to Reagan and Bush, despite all the grief they took from a mainstream media labeling them delirious and dangerous.

You may find it surprising after the avalanche of Fake News about me, but there were monuments to me, as well. Big, beautiful monuments, and I don't just mean Jeroboam's Wall. You couldn't have guessed it from what you read in a Bible whose historical sections were produced by Jeroboam-haters, but monuments there were to me in abundance. True, your archaeologists haven't found them yet, but they will, eventually. Keep digging. They are all there, hidden yet beneath the sands of time.

Not that I needed monuments, you understand. My favorite place in St. Paul's Cathedral in London is the corner of the crypt where is buried the cathedral's architect and builder, Christopher Wren. The church is filled with monumental monuments to the likes of the Duke of Wellington astride Copenhagen and to Horatio, Lord Nelson, killed in the Battle of Trafalgar in Spain.

But down below, in a corner of the crypt midst all the monuments and statues, the tomb for the architect of the cathedral is a simple plaque with a Latin inscription: *Lector, si monumentum requiris, circumspice.* It means, *"Reader, if you require a monument, look around you."*

Sad that no mention was made in the Bible of my funeral, only a bare note of my death after reigning in Israel for 22 years. So utterly anti-Jeroboam is the text that it is understandable should the lector, the reader, imagine I was shuffled into an anonymous grave, the tyrant at last meeting his ignominious end, something like the Wicked Witch of the West. *"I'm melting, I'm melting, I'm melting into history! What a world! What a cruel world!"*

That was not the case. My funeral was a majestic moment in our nation's history when the people truly mourned, and I don't mean paid mourners like Herod the Great had when he was buried at Herodian. No, my people mourned me as a truly great king who had *Made Israel Great Again*, despite the ceaseless ranting of critics, intent on painting my every decision in the worst possible light.

So, I say with Sir Christopher Wren, *Look Around You*! I was the architect of Israel's prosperity and from what I am seeing, your President Trump is accomplishing the same. *Look around you!* Good things are happening. Stay calm and enjoy the ride!

CHAPTER THIRTEEN

One More Thing

———

Jedediah: As we come near the end of our time tonight, I should explain to our many viewers who may not be not regular viewers of *The Five* that one of our most popular features comes at the end of each episode. We call it *One More Thing*, each of our hosts introducing a curious news item, mostly trivial, from that day's news.

Tonight, for our *One More Thing* segment, I want to go to our special guests one last time to ask what character in the Bible does your host most remind you of?

I'll start with you, Ahijah. We all think of Juan as Methuselah, the only one of us old enough for Medicare. Does that work for you as you think of Juan?

Ahijah: Oh, no, Jedediah, not at all Methuselah. I've met Methuselah. Methuselah is a friend of mine and I can tell you, Juan, you're no Methuselah!

I'm kidding, of course. It's a great question, Jedediah. I said earlier that today's Democrats, progressives, are akin to prophets, fervent in their call for social justice. Juan Williams, my gracious host, reminds me of none other than the Prophet Micah, who wrote, *"He hath shown thee, O man, what is good: and what doth the Lord require of thee but to do justly and to love mercy, and to walk humbly with thy God?"*

That, I think, summarizes the life and work of such an eloquent Democrat as Juan Williams. I see him as the Gentleman Prophet, calling his nation to such policies that will lift all Americans and especially the disadvantaged.

Jedediah: Thank you, Mr. Prophet, we all love Juan and agree that he is passionate about causes that better lives, even though we might, but only occasionally, disagree with him.

Okay, then, what about our Dana? Zerlinda, what Bible story tells Dana's story?

Zerlinda: My hostess, Dana, is beautiful inside and out, and strong. She is able to pull off standing for her conservative principles while, at the same time, displaying such kindness and fairness that she clearly is respected, even embraced, by both sides of today's political argument. She strikes me as the epitome of Fox's *"Fair and Balanced"* mantra.

Her wisdom and strength led her to become the second White House spokesperson during the George W. Bush presidency, so I will have to choose a biblical woman who liked the microphone. That's why I say that Dana reminds me of Miriam, the sister of Moses and Aaron. She was wise, passionate, and eloquent. One of the most beautiful passages in all of scripture is her *Shirat ha-Yam*, the Song of the Sea. It's found in Exodus 15 after Israel crossed the Red Sea on dry land. *"I will sing to the LORD, for he has triumphed gloriously; horse and rider he has thrown into the sea. The LORD is my strength and my might and he has become my salvation."*

Jedediah: Thank you, Zerlinda. Dana as Miriam. I like it. What about you Nebat? Who does Greg remind you of in the Bible?

Nebat: Ah, there is no doubt, Jedediah, Greg would be a natural to play the patriarch Jacob. A trickster with monologues smooth and cunning. The name Jacob in Hebrew basically means "conman," but I don't mean that in a bad way, Greg, though I think you could talk anybody out of anything, just as Jacob talked his twin brother Esau out of his birthright.

One of my favorite Bible stories is Jacob running away from his father-in-law Laban with his wife, Rachel. Laban catches up to the AWOL Jacob at a place called Mizpah. After negotiations, when they part ways, they share what is known as the Mizpah blessing, *"May the Lord watch between me and thee when we are apart one from another."*

It sounds like such a wonderful benediction, a parting of caring. But, what is actually being said is, *"May the Lord watch you when I can't see you, because I don't trust you as far as I could throw you."* That sums it up. That's Greg, a bit on the cynical side!

Jedediah: Greg as Jacob, I get it! What about you, King Jeroboam? Who is Jesse?

Jeroboam: I was thinking also of Jacob for Jesse and for similar reasons. But since Jacob is taken, I'll choose Absalom, who, a generation before I did the same, won over the hearts of Israel's tribes. Absalom, David's son, rebelled against his father King David, just as I rebelled against King Solomon, Absalom's half-brother.

Why Absalom? Well, he was smooth and very charismatic, like Jesse. He stirred rebellion by going out to the people in the tribes, particularly the northern tribes whom I eventually won over. He would listen to their complaints and at last say, *"Oh, I hear you, I hear you. I feel your pain! If only I was king in the land, I would address your grievances."*

It all reminds me of *Watter's World*, Absalom's going out to the people to establish a connection. Absalom is the oleaginous Eddie Haskell of the Bible. *"Gee, Mrs. Cleaver, you sure look nice today!"* Such smarminess, pure flattery and ingratiation, can get you places! It's not a waste, and I think Jesse would make a great Absalom, slick in just the right measure. Oh, and, great hair! Absalom also had great hair, and you can look that up!

Jedediah: I love it! Well, that leaves only Queen Ano, seated by me. As she ended our first hour, I'll leave it to her to end our second hour. Dare I ask? Who do I remind you of?

Ano: When I came to Israel as queen, Jedediah, one of the first places I visited was Mount Tabor, at the edge of the Jezreel Valley, a portion of the land held by the ten tribes. I learned that it was here at Mt. Tabor that, during the time of the Judges, Deborah had defeated the Canaanites under the command of General Sisera from Hazor, a major Canaanite city further north in the Galilee.

Jedediah would make a good Deborah, strong and victorious, but when I look at Jedediah I see in her not so much Deborah as Jael, the Kenite woman who gave sanctuary to the Canaanite general during the battle, then disposed of him in a gruesome way, with a tent peg and a mallet.

Deborah sings of her victory, "*Most blessed of women be Jael, the wife of Heber the Kenite, of tent-dwelling women most blessed. He asked for water and she gave him milk, she brought him curds in a lordly bowl. She put her hand to the tent peg and her right hand to the workman's mallet, she struck Sisera a blow, she crushed his head, she shattered and pierced his temple. He sank, he fell, he lay still at her feet. At her feet he sank, he fell, where he sank, he fell dead.*"

Goodness, I hate to end your show on a bloody note, but don't panic, Jedediah. Jael was no common murderer, but a hero. She made a risky political choice which was totally unexpected, just as Jedediah has done.

Also, I love it that Jael means ibex, or wild goat (which, as I think of it, perhaps Jael should have been Mr. "Animals are Great," Greg Gutfeld). In the ibex I see skill and energy, not to mention beauty. So I say Jael for Jedediah, J for J, the beautiful and the brave. Jedediah is made of such stuff, the Pundit Warrior, the slayer of liberalism!

Jesse: And that's all we have time for, folks. Thanks for joining us on this special edition of *The Five*, which has been tonight, and tonight only, *The Ten*. See you tomorrow at five, and now here's Bret with *Special Report*.

THE AUTHOR'S CONCLUSION

As Jesse introduced Bret Baier I stirred from my nap, gradually rousing from that wonderfully in-between place, the mandorla threshold one crosses when emerging from the dusk of sleep to the re-dawning of awareness. My glass of red long empty, as I walked to the kitchen for a refill I reflected upon my dream, it not yet as erased from my memory as had been the wine from my glass.

Being a conservative, politically and biblically, I had always assumed Jeroboam ben Nebat to be precisely what the Bible says he was, evil, never thinking to question the biblical injunctions against him. Is it possible that a 3,000 year old story from the Hebrew Bible might better be understood in the light of today's venomous political climate? Perhaps so, for if Donald J. Trump rose to power promising to "Build the Wall" and to "Drain the Swamp," hadn't Jeroboam ben Nebat accomplished precisely the same? Had not his altar become a "Wall" to restrict pilgrims from crossing the border to Jerusalem? Had not his replacement of the established Levitical priesthood with his own representatives drained what he had come to regard as a swamp within Solomon's powerful Deep State?

These thoughts led me to wonder, had my defense of Donald J. Trump for these two very things opened my mind to look at the Bible's description of Jeroboam with a different eye? Could it really be that the Bible's historians reported on Jeroboam's reign in the same deranged way I daily witness CNN and MSNBC reporting on the presidency of Donald J. Trump?

To be sure, my dream of Israel's first king, Jeroboam ben Nebat, was only a fantasy of my Cabernet slumber, but it rang true, if only in that Jeroboam would have had his side of the story to tell, as would his father, mother, and wife. The Bible doesn't let us to hear their stories, allowing us only to judge them through the prescribed lens of orthodoxy, their side of history erased from the biblical narrative so completely that it has been unheard for three thousand years, and will forever remain unheard.

So while my dream has been just that, a fantasy untethered from reality, perhaps my imagination of how he might tell his story, were he given an opportunity after three millennia to do so, will serve as a reminder that he deserves an opportunity to defend himself against the historical assessment rendered by the biblical writers. I doubt I would ever have given the king a voice to defend himself against the biblical narrative had I not observed almost daily in these past two years a certain *Trump Derangement Syndrome* fashioning the Left's narrative of the presidency of Donald J. Trump. If the mainstream media can so profoundly shape our views of today's news, doesn't it stand to reason that the same holds true in the shaping of our broader assessment of historical figures?

Not long after I began to write *Jeroboam Derangement Syndrome*, the story of the Covington Kids broke. Several of my Facebook friends immediately jumped on board the mainstream media narrative, posting assaults on Trump's supporters alongside the image of a MAGA hat-wearing sixteen-year old from Covington Catholic High School in Kentucky, he staring down a native American-Indian Vietnam veteran. The message was crystal clear: "How is it possible that you who support this illegitimate president can't see what evil he is bringing to our country?" I read their posts, as repulsed as they by the picture and, as any rational person, found myself ashamed of those kids' for their vile actions.

Soon enough, though, the "other side" of the story came out, again shattering trust in today's mainstream media. When the longer video surfaced, offering a fuller accounting of how the ugly event had actually transpired, it at least softened, if not entirely vindicated, the Covington Kids. Clearly the truth, which would have had been easily accessible, had been ignored due to the bias of an Establishment media gone delirious with the slightest scent of Trumpian blood in the water.

In the pre-technological era of Jeroboam, three thousand years ago, the Covington Kids would have been without defense, entirely at the mercy of the established venues of opinion-makers, the words of the prophets and the ink of the scribes. That, thankfully, is no longer the case, a fact from which the mainstream media is still staggering, recognizing their loss of control. How, otherwise, they wonder, could a man like Donald J. Trump have been elected? How else could this man have stayed in office as the media has relentlessly attacked, charging at every potential news item which might render his presidency vulnerable?

With that, I leave my dream to the reader to assess if the similarities between Jeroboam ben Nebat and Donald J. Trump point to two rulers separated by 3,000 years who are equally deficient or even criminal, or do they point to two media equally crazed and deranged? Perhaps, if we are willing to listen, we will discover that the truth is not either/or, but an amalgam more nuanced than our supposed self-sureties might lead us to believe.

As I introduced my dream with John Bunyan's literary classic, *The Pilgrim's Progress*, so I close with a small portion of his Conclusion:

> *Now, reader, I have told my dream to thee . . .*
>
> *What of my dross thou findest there, be bold*
>
> *To throw away, but yet preserve the gold;*
>
> *What if my gold be wrapped up in ore?*
>
> *None throws away the apple for the core.*
>
> *But if thou shalt cast away all as vain,*
>
> *I know not but 'twill make me dream again.*